REVENANT

Book Two of The Lychos Cycle

PATTI LARSEN

ALSO BY

PATTI LARSEN

The Hayle Coven Universe

The Hunted Series
Fiona Fleming Cozy Mysteries
The Nightshade Cases
The Clone Chronicles
The Diamond City Trilogy
Didi and the Gunslinger

and much, much more.
Find your new favorite author at
pattilarsen.com
Sign up for new releases
bit.ly/pattilarsenemail

ONE

Sage stumbles over the threshold. The culprit, torn carpeting come loose from the metal strip holding it down. A faint odor rises to my sensitive nose with each step, memories of all the feet that have passed down this hall, to this room we've lied to rent.

He manages to right himself as I slip the door shut behind us. His sea-green eyes meet mine, lips trying to smile around a grimace of pain as my shoulder brushes his when I turn to support him. Damn it, the left side, where the bite festers under his jacket. The bite that's led us here, to this run-down hotel in the heart of Kiev.

I ease him down on the creaking bed, trying not to think of what might be living under the thin sheets, the spotted comforter, in the heart of the mattress. Since when did a few bugs and a bit of dirt disgust me so?

There were times I resided in moldering piles of straw for weeks at a stretch with stale water and no food to sustain me, coated in my own filth, nose burned out from the cutting odor of ammonia. Hunting rats and small insects was my only means of sustenance and staying alive at all costs my animal-instinct.

How easily I've forgotten my humble and terrible beginnings. I've become soft as princess of the werenation, far-gone from the girl who would do anything to survive. I can't afford to be weak, coddled, arrogant in my position and blind to the suffering, which made me who I am. Not if I'm going to save Sage from certain death.

He doesn't audibly complain of the pain, but it shows on his face. He pulls me down beside him with his right hand, keeping me on his good side. His strong fingers lace through mine, a smile finally lifting the corners of his shapely lips.

"I always wanted to visit Kiev," he says. "I just didn't expect it to be like this."

It's so hard for me not to hug him, rock him like an injured child. I have to resist weakness now, in all forms. The girl I used to be cared for others, had friends, to a point, as much as such things were allowed by the Black Soul sorcerers who owned my people. Before she was given away to the Dumonts and taught a whole new kind of life, where pain and degradation ruled and any rebellion was met with agony. She understands what I need to do. Who I have to be if Sage is to survive. But I can't quite bring myself to accept her, holding her at arm's length within. It may mean our downfall. Still, I've come so far since she huddled in a cage like an animal, waiting for her next punishment, never breaking, not once.

I hope I can draw on what she has to offer, what my wolf has to offer, without reverting to the savage and hate-filled young thing I outgrew.

It might be harder than I think. We are on our own, hunted by the werenation, thanks to Sage's revenant status. I've thrown everything away to save him, to be with him. But I'm not alone this time. My cage is the whole world, and Sage is with me. My love is beside me. And I will not allow my choice to lead to failure, even if it means giving in to old hate to see him safe.

Magic that feels like Enforcers brushes the edges of the shields I maintain around us. My power protects us, at least for now. But the longer we remain in Ukraine, the more likely it is we will be discovered. I imagine my dear friend, Sydlynn Hayle, is also searching, though her plans for Sage and I don't involve putting him to death for being a revenant. I squeeze Sage's hand as I reach for his jacket and push it back away from his left shoulder to examine the wound.

The skin is red, infection likely as faint lines run

outward from the bite. The teeth of his attacker bit deep, small chunks of skin flapped over two of the punctures, puffy and oozing clear fluid. The imprint is wide, as far across as my splayed hand. It's the bite of a werewolf, though Sage still swears it was a smaller version, a real wolf, not the half-transformed shape my people and I take when we shift. But it's impossible a wolf bit him, not with the were infection spreading through his system. He must have seen one thing and his brain translated it into another out of a sheer lack of ability to process.

He hisses as I touch the edge of the bite, barely applying any kind of pressure. I lean back, grim, but doing my best not to show my worry. I'll have to feed him antibiotics or find some other medicine to treat him. I smell the taint of the revenant, but it's faint, like a distant memory more than a current threat. Normal revenants—humans bitten by werewolves—have a stink about them that makes them flawed and oh-so-obvious to pureborns like me. I have my suspicions about the reason for the bite victim's loss of humanity and madness. Perhaps it's the lack of magic in the victim to support the wolf transferred in the bite. Being born a werewolf means having genes and power passed down from at least one parent. But when a normal is bitten, there is no such transfer. Only the infectious illness of the werewolf legacy.

But despite my worries about him, Sage doesn't

carry the heavy stench of the revenants I've dealt with in the past. Mind you, the first one I met was when I was only a little girl, but my nose never forgets a scent. The recent outbreak of revenants the European Witch Council has been tracking carry the same familiar odor, refreshing my nasal memory and making me hyper-sensitive to it in Sage.

Which makes me think of Caine and his people. I know it was his teeth that made the bite dooming Sage to this fate. I have no proof, but my heart knows the truth, the smirk of satisfaction he shared with me all the confession I need. Regardless, Cicero Caine and his pack from California are no born-and-bred werewolves themselves. I am also certain they are revenants, created by sorcerers, though whether it's the renewed rise of the Brotherhood behind this, or some other sect I have yet to encounter, they have somehow managed to create werewolves where once only the Black Souls who made my people had that power.

While our former masters, too, were sorcerers, the process they used to make my people was a closely guarded secret in their ranks, known only to the members of their order. The Black Souls had remained outside the political conflicts of the Brotherhood and the Steam Union, the two official sides of the sorcerous sects. Suspicious and devious, the Black Souls order kept themselves apart, ruling northern Europe with an iron grip and the darkness of their power, through our influence as their army. If it weren't for Sydlynn Hayle, we would be under their thumb even yet.

I believed the process of creating new werewolves had been lost with the fall of the evil men who owned my people. Now I'm not so sure.

A cure must exist. If werewolves can be made, if the infection my people carry can be transferred to normals, there has to be a way to heal it. My dear Syd, and others I call friend, has already tried and failed. But the sorcerer who succeeded in making Caine and his pack must have the answer.

And I intend to find it before seven days pass and Sage turns into a mindless savage.

"We need to keep moving." Sage shifts restlessly beside me, my fingers releasing the edge of his jacket, hiding the wound. I need to, at the very least, acquire bandages so he doesn't seep through his clothing. I don't want normals to start noticing he's not well and ask questions I don't have time to make up lies to cover.

"You need rest," I say, releasing his hand, rising to stand over him. "And I have to talk to someone." There's a reason we're here, in Kiev, and not miles closer to the border by now. The werewolf palace, the center of our nation, lies north and east, almost on the Russian border. We have limited time, only a week if the report Femke Svennson, the leader of the European High Council, can be believed. We've already lost one to his capture and my rescue of him, followed by our flight here. But we need resources and there is only one person I can think of who might supply them.

Might. Either that or I'm going to a fight I might not win. But I have to risk it.

Sage tries to join me, but I push him down gently.

"You're not going without me." How I love the way his jaw sets in stubbornness, the flash of defiance in his eyes. Is that his wolf waking? But no, he's always had those traits, only well hidden under kindness and his sense of humor he wears like a cloak.

"Where I go," I say, bending to kiss his forehead, "you cannot come, Sage. Please, believe me. I'll return soon. Sleep or, at the very least, lie down and close your eyes. You'll need your strength when I return."

He hesitates. "Won't they find me if you're gone?" Clever, so clever, my darling Sage. "You said you were using your magic to hide me." I love how he's adapted so smoothly, accepted this new reality he finds himself in without real complaint. It might be innocence or a form of deflection for him, but I can't let anything happen to hurt him. Not now, not ever.

"They won't," I say. "I'm not going far and my shielding will hold." At least, I assume that's the case. I have no way of knowing, but I can't bring him with me where I'm going. I just have to risk it.

He finally nods. "Where are you going?"

"We need passports," I say, heading for the door. "Money and other papers. I know someone in the city who can get them for us."

Sage's scent turns to fear. "You're talking about the Mafia." He thought originally that was the secret of my past I hid from him. He learned better when he was bitten, confronted with magic and werewolves and laws beyond his norm.

I smile back at him, one hand on the rusting door knob. "I am," I say. "But who do you think should be afraid—them or me?"

He manages a little grin, shakes his head. "I wouldn't cross you."

I laugh and leave the room, briefly leaning my forehead against the door as I close it behind me. Only then does my own fear surface, out of his view.

Risky, this option. My contact here is untrustworthy. But I have no choice. If we are to escape Europe and make it to America, I have to travel under the radar. Which means no magic.

Which means... I pull away from the door and spin, heading for the creaking stairs in the dimly lit and grungy hallway.

If my contact won't give me what I want, I'll take it. Or die trying.

TWO

The front of the restaurant is gaudy, the paint bright red and gold, the colors of Mother Russia. But it's chintzy, old and unrepaired. A dive, Syd would call it. I keep my head down, blonde hair covered in a black wool toque, hands shoved in the pockets of my leather jacket. Night has fallen, the crisp air feeling of approaching winter, though it's only late September. This close to the Russian border, snow comes early enough.

The street is bustling, making my approach all the easier, the stink of cigar smoke and stale furs brought out of mothballed storage wafting around me. My boots make no sound on the pavement as I weave through the crowd to the restaurant front, eyes carefully observing the two hulking men outside the front door. Standard Mafia bodyguards in long, black leather jackets, one bald, the other dyed blond with shoulders as wide as the doorway. I don't have to look for bulges under their clothing. They are armed, no question.

The only good thing about their presence? My target is exactly where I expected him to be. He uses this place as his personal office, claiming to be a fan of the traditional Ukrainian *borshch*. I know better—his territory surrounds him here, his base of power strongest in this neighborhood.

I can't show hesitation. Instead, I continue at the same ground-eating pace, striding up to the front of the restaurant. The two bullies tense as I approach, attempting to intimidate, but I flash my wolf eyes at the bald one closest to me, barely a glance upward. He flinches, nods and steps aside, allowing me to enter.

The normal guards of the Mafia know us. And still fear werewolves, it seems.

I hoped as much.

I step into a dark interior, a few globe lights tinted with red tissue paper hanging over the tables dressed in hideous and ancient cloths. The filthy carpet swishes under my boots, sweet and sour mixing with more cigar smoke and the spicy scent of vodka. Normals claim vodka has little to no aroma, but to werewolves, it fills our noses with spikes.

A thin girl with stringy brown hair hovers beside the center table. I see her shaking hands from where I stand, though she doesn't seem to be in danger. Especially not from the lone man sitting at the table, leaned back in his chair, balding head threaded around with long, black hair he uses to try to hide his loss. Round cheeks lift into cherub-like pink cherries as he spots me.

"Sharlotta!" He gestures with one thick-fingered hand, the ember on the end of his fat cigar glowing bright as it swishes through the air. I pinch back a scowl at the use of my formal name. He's taunting me. The girl looks up at me, panic on her face as I approach at a slower pace. Her eyes widen, fear increasing. He reaches out and pats the girl's hand as though to reassure her, only making her jump. "A bowl of *borshch*!" His jovial tone doesn't reach the glittering darkness of his watchful eyes. "Two!"

The serving girl dashes off, her apron flapping, skirt twisting around her thin legs. I ignore her, focusing on the man before me as he rises. He grasps my arms in both hands, a curl of cigar smoke climbing to my face as he kisses my cheeks, one after the other, with enthusiasm.

"Iosif." I hold still as he beams at me. "You look well."

He preens a little, sliding his empty hand across his temple, thick mustache dancing over his crooked teeth. "And you, sweet Charlotte," he says in softly accented English. "But things must be desperate for you to come to Iosif Greshnev's door." He sits, gesturing for me to do the same. I sink slowly into a chair, hands still in my pockets. The girl arrives, sets a bowl in front of me, the edge rattling as she releases at the last moment, red juice sloshing over one side.

Iosif curses at her in Russian before sending her scrambling. "New girl," he grunts, lifting a giant spoon full of the meaty beet soup to his lips. The edge of the spoon catches his mustache, the black hair wet. I ignore mine, the scent of meat and vegetables strong in the dark red bowl. I'm not here to eat.

Iosif leans back, still chewing, taking a long pull from his cigar. The vest he wears under his suit jacket strains, the buttons tight over his growing belly. I assess him in a quick once-over, the expensive fabric, the shine of the diamond on his right hand, the silk of his loosened tie, the Cuban label on his cigar. Iosif has always been powerful and popular in the Mafia, but I can tell he's risen in the ranks since we last spoke.

"You need me." He laughs out loud, left hand coming down hard enough on the table to make my soup jump. "After all this time, after your supposed freedom, you and your grandfather," there is no bitterness in his tone, at least, so I don't tense just yet, "you need me."

I nod. There's no use lying about it. "I do."

Iosif looks startled a moment before leaning forward. He expected me to lie, but doing so will only prolong this dance with him. I've only ever seen calculation and craftiness in his eyes before. I worked for him long ago, because of the Dumonts, assisting in their illegal activities through the Russian mob. Though Iosif had always dealt fairly with me—something I knew was a rarity in the organization—he, never the less, was born and bred to this life as much as I was to mine.

Why then do I now see compassion and a hint of worry in his expression? Or am I merely fooling myself?

"Well then," he says, taking another draw from his cigar. "Tell me what I can do for you, princess."

How much do I tell him? I'd rather keep it small and swift, but Iosif has always been clever beyond all appearances and I know he will give me trouble if I hold anything back from him. So, I unfold the story in its entirety, including Femke Svennson's fears about the revenants and my own fugitive status. I'm quite sure, with his connections, he knows most of it anyway.

He grunts a time or two as I speak, but doesn't interrupt. When I'm done, my hands are free and flat on the table before me, my eyes going to the deep crimson depths of my cooling soup.

"There are those among the organization," he says, "who have passed word of such troubling happenings." He's nodding, almost to himself. "I assured the concerned parties it has nothing to do with you or your people." Dark eyes hold nothing but quiet, though that in itself is a warning. "The concerned parties," his bosses, no doubt, "wish to take action if such instances continue to surface." Coming from anyone else, I would take his words as a threat. But Iosif is trying to help me, of that I'm certain. He smells like worry to me. "I can hold them off with a word from you the werenation is tackling the problem head on."

I nod. "Assuredly," I say.

He smiles suddenly, before his eyes tighten around the edges. "These Californian werewolves," Iosif says, words light, almost soft. "I've heard of them, as well."

My turn to be surprised. "Anything I can use?"

He shrugs, thick-fingered hands patting the table cloth. "They are based out of Los Angeles," he says. "First contact with the family came from that city." And now I have a specific location. Excellent. This visit to Iosif has already been worth it with that one tidbit. The light shines on his ring as he points at me. "Know this, princess of the werenation. Even those above," he now jabs over his head, though I know he means his bosses, "are wary of hiring them, despite their desire to possess such assets again."

"They've been approached?" How long have Caine and his pack been here in Europe? Far longer than a few days in Yutsk, obviously.

"Briefly," Iosif says with a sigh. "But their leader…there is something wrong with him, my dear."

I nod. "Now you know why."

Iosif doesn't say anything. For a long time we sit

there, him smoking his cigar, watching me. I hold still, waiting. He's heard everything, knows what I'm after. He will either help or he won't.

"You say you seek a cure." A wreath of smoke masks his features as he speaks, voice soft and flat. "What if there is no such thing?"

"There is," I say, without doubt.

Iosif sighs out a large puff, the scent carrying its cloying breath to me. "The Black Souls created a terrible legacy," he says. I'm actually startled he knows about them. I assumed he thought the Dumonts were our masters. I should know better than to underestimate Iosif. "You wish to make him human again?"

I nod, though I will take anything. "That is the hope."

Iosif sets aside his cigar. "And if the alternative is to somehow make him a werewolf, like you?"

It's not possible. Even if Sage were to make it through the revenant process, to become like Caine and his pack, he will never be a trueborn werewolf. Never. But will it be enough for me, if Sage makes it that far, if he maintains his sanity? Can I live with that?

The alternative is his death. And once the werenation finds him, only death will be his fate. It is law.

"Do you know more you're not telling me?" I keep my tone mild, though I want to leap over the table at Iosif and strangle it out of him.

"Perhaps." He pushes aside his bowl, no longer steaming. The crimson fluid sloshes, like thinned blood on the white porcelain. "Might I offer this single shred of hope." He doesn't meet my eyes. "Werewolves weren't born. They were first created. Ask yourself what makes you so different from the boy you protect, in the end."

A flare of unbidden pride hits me. I was born a werewolf, I'm no revenant. And yet, Iosif is correct. We, all of the werenation, are descended from revenants. An interesting thought, that.

"I will supply what you need," Iosif says abruptly, leaning forward again to take one of my hands in his. The gold band holding his diamond feels hot, his thick fingers, too. "But there are things you must know, my dear."

I can't help but tilt my head to the side, a wolfish thing to do. "Tell me."

"There is a price on your head." He flashes another crooked-toothed smile. "Quite a sizeable one. And the boy you're traveling with. If I wasn't rich, I'd be tempted."

I simply nod. "You knew what I told you already."

"Some of it." He snaps his fingers. The kitchen door opens and his two bodyguards enter. They have Sage between them. I don't react. I can't show Iosif weakness, but if they have harmed him, I will kill them all.

Iosif pats my hand. "Fear not," he says. "You were honest with me, Charlotte." I note he's returned to my more common name, the one the Dumonts used for me, and feel myself relax because of it. "And I respect that. I've always respected you." He shrugs. "The folly of an old man, perhaps, to trust a were. But I do." He laughs, a coughing sound filled with years of cigar smoke. "Imagine that, a *mafiya* man like me, trusting a pretty young beast like you." He pats his round belly, watching me with those narrow, dark eyes. "Perhaps I'm too trusting. But after all you've done for me in the past, you deserve a chance to see this through."

How kind of him. And yet, his trust isn't returned, not completely. "What's your price?" There is always a price.

Iosif laughs while Sage comes to my side. His hand is shaking as he sets it on my shoulder, but he feels relatively calm, so I keep focused on the man in the suit next to me. "Always about business with you, princess." He points at my soup. "Eat some *borshch* while my people put your papers together."

I shake my head, pushing the plate away, ready to walk. "The price, Iosif."

He sighs, seems to deflate. "Perhaps I just want to help you," he says. And then winks with a glitter in his eyes. "For old time's sake. Or perhaps I will enjoy knowing the princess of the werewolves owes me a favor."

And he'll collect one day, I have no doubt. I offer

my hand without hesitation, regardless. I don't have a choice otherwise. "Deal."

We shake as Sage takes a seat next to me, frowning. "Sage America," I say, "this is Iosif Greshnev."

Sage looks back and forth between us. "Nice to meet you."

Iosif laughs again, robust and loud. "You say that now," he says. "Oh, my dear," he turns to me. "I've always admired you and your family. Your darling mother. Your impetuous brother. But only you, Sharlotta, would put your life and everything you have in danger for a normal." He winks again. "And that, dear girl, is the real reason I'm helping you."

THREE

I sit in the back of a non-descript van, unheated and bare to the steel floor. The windows have been painted over, the only light coming through the front windshield. Sage huddles next to me, shivering, favoring his shoulder. The two guards from the restaurant watch over us, one with a machine gun in his lap, the other cradling a handgun.

Sage turns his head, lips next to my ear. "Who are these people?"

I don't answer. He already knows, doesn't he?

"Am I the only one who thinks this is a bad idea?" He doesn't sound petulant, or complaining. Just solidly anxious, though his old strength runs through him, keeping his voice steady, his whole being poised for action.

"No," I say. "But we are fugitives and they are the only resource I have to win our freedom."

"We could go back." Sage's hand reaches for mine, squeezes my cold fingers as the lights of the city flash past the windshield, the cold dark and quiet of the countryside ahead. "You have a bigger destiny, Charlie. And I'm getting in the way."

"So you want to die." I'm feeling blunt, to the point. Unwilling to pull punches. He needs to understand this sacrifice isn't just about him.

"No," he says. "But if I'm going to turn into some kind of monster and start making others like me, I guess the answer would be yes."

"There's no guarantee of that," I say, hoping I'm right. His scent remains pure of the revenant taint, even a full day after being bitten, so my hope is stronger than maybe it should be. "For all we know, you won't devolve. And until you prove to me you will, I'm going to work on the assumption there is a way to help you, if you don't mind."

Sage's teeth flash in the single streetlight as he smiles at me. "Whatever you say, princess."

I would hit him, but I'm too amused. A strange place and time to find humor, but I'm not one to discard the chance to lighten the mood if it makes him feel better.

Sage dozes on my shoulder as the hours pass. Iosif promised his men would take us to the border of

Slovakia, bribe our way across. It was the best he could do, but it will mean we are out of Ukraine and, with the new papers in our possession, it's enough.

I refuse to worry what I now owe the Mafia leader. He's no Ukrainian, Russian by birth, from what I understand. But unlike other Russian leaders, he has adapted to our country, made himself comfortable, adopted us as his own. The cold and terrible emptiness in the hearts of other Mafia leaders I've met is absent in Iosif. He is either an excellent actor—able to fool even a werewolf—or he genuinely cares for the people. An odd combination for a man steeped in organized crime. His own code of ethics could get him in trouble one day.

I will be there on that day to make sure he is the victorious one for what he's done for Sage and me.

A pothole jars the van, lifting me from the floor slightly, slamming me back down again. Sage surges awake, a growl on his lips. He turns to face me as the two guards cock their weapons, looking suddenly fearful. As they should. Sage's eyes have gone wolf.

I turn toward him, reaching for him with my magic, fear surging in my heart. Is this the time, when the revenant begins to show? Were we in the palace, he would be dragged from his cell and to the throne room, to be beheaded and then cast upon a pyre to burn to dust. But he's here, with me, and if I've chosen wrong, it's possible the two guards will die for my foolishness.

But when I fix my gaze and power upon Sage, I realize there is no madness in him. The wolf has risen, barely to the surface, a reaction to being startled. But he is sane and present, the scent of him as fresh as ever, though now filled with the musky depth of a wolf.

His snarl retreats, dark eyes returning to their sea green, my own canine vision crisp even in the low light.

"Sorry," he mutters, shaking his head. "What happened?"

I laugh nervously, just for his ears, before glaring at the two Mafia guards. They are shaking, eyes wide. Iosif must have warned them about Sage. Did he give orders to kill us both if my love began to turn? I wouldn't be surprised, despite his claims of trust. He has his "concerned parties" to worry about, after all.

"He's fine," I say, cold, commanding. "Cowards."

That raises frowns, anger. The bald one uncocks his handgun, though he remains stiff, while his friend looks forward toward the driver.

"How long?" His Ukrainian is rough, uncultured. Another foreigner in my country. I shake off my irritation and listen for the reply.

"Two more miles." The driver is a slim man with a ragged scar on his cheek. He chain-smokes filterless cigarettes, his window wide open to the cold. I shiver and pull Sage to me, feeling his wolf retreat until it is gone.

The bald guard nods to me. "The border," he says

in even harsher Ukrainian.

I wave him off, speaking Russian so I don't have to listen to him butcher my mother tongue with his uncouth mouth. "We're ready." My new backpack rests behind me, a softer place to lean on than the cold wall of the van.

They seem more than happy to see us go. And the feeling is completely mutual.

I peer over the driver's shoulder, nose flaring at the heavy scent of smoke, wolf's gaze catching the distant glimmer of lights signaling the border crossing.

"Arrangements have been made," the driver says in a cheerful tone. He, at least, is Ukrainian, judging by his accent. "This will be but a moment."

I nod, begin to sit back, before freezing in place when I feel them against my shielding.

Enforcers. I jerk back into position, eyes narrowing, searching the sky over the rapidly approaching border. They are nowhere in sight, but I sense the pressure of their power. Femke is looking for us.

For a moment, I consider turning us in. At least Femke will be fair, treat Sage with courtesy and kindness. But she is bound by law, and will have no choice but to return us to my grandfather. So, no. We must avoid her Enforcers at all costs.

"Stop." The driver is startled, drops his cigarette with a curse, slamming on the brakes at the grating sound of my voice in his ear. "We must get out here."

The bald guard joins me behind the driver's seat. "What is it?"

I shake my head, turning to Sage who stares at me with growing anxiety.

"Nothing you can help us with," I say as I lunge for Sage and our backpacks. "Tell Iosif thank you. Your duty is done."

The back of the van opens easily under my hands, the well-oiled hinges telling me we're not the first ones forced to sneak out before the journey is over. The bald guard slips out the back with us, breath rising from his lips in a column of mist as he points off to the right.

"Tsurl," he says. "Small town, you can hide there."

I look to the left. "And that way?"

"Train tracks." He shrugs, washing his hands of us as he leaps into the back of the van and pulls the doors shut.

I pull Sage off the rutted road as the van makes a U-turn, the driver waving a jaunty farewell with his glowing cigarette. Tall grass and brush are an excellent hiding place in the dark, but only for a short time. I glance up the road toward the border, waiting to see if the van's departure has been noticed.

Nothing, no movement. And the Enforcer presence is steady, as though waiting, not actively searching. So we are in no worse shape now than before.

Sage shoulders his pack, turning right, toward town.

But I'm already slinking across the road, heading left. He hurries to catch up with me, hand on my arm. "Where are we going?"

"Enforcers are waiting for us at the border." Fcmkc has to uphold law, even werelaw. The magical safety of Europe is her responsibility and having Sage running around—a known revenant in her territory—means she's now forced to pursue us. Sage grimaces, looks back over his shoulder. "We'll find a way across." I pull him along by his grip on me, feeling his hand slide down to take mine. "But, for now, I don't feel like walking, do you?" He shakes his head. "Then let's go catch a train."

FOUR

The train is the perfect choice, at least. And Sage surprises me in how easily and courageously he boards the slow-moving boxcar. We luck out. The section of track near the border is curved and steep, offering an excellent opportunity for us to board safely. When I grin at him from the dark of the boxcar after a daring leap, he grins back.

"Not my first time traveling," he says.

We settle among piles of boxes on the steel floor, a large sheet of discarded cardboard our only cushion, but enough to keep the chill of the metal from seeping through and into us. I position myself with a clear view of the partially open door, eyes locked on the horizon rolling past. Sage rummages through the bag Iosif gave him, snuffling at the foil-wrapped bundle he pulls free before his eyes light up.

He manages to control his hunger long enough to offer me some of his roast beef sandwich, the bread thick and homemade, fresh cut from the smell, but I wave him off, amused by the relief in his smile as he devours his meal. I'm certain another sandwich hides in my own bag, but I'll save it for later. I'm far too tense to enjoy food right now and Sage might need it later.

Sage finally slips back, resting his shoulders against a box, pressed against me, sighing softly as he brushes crumbs from his jacket. "Man, I've never been so starved."

I don't comment, though worry pings. Young werewolves are often voracious eaters. I then have to remind myself he's not a werewolf at all, but a human turning revenant. That just adds to my anxiety.

I hardly needed the reminder.

Sage's hand slips around mine, fingers warm through the leather of my glove despite the cool evening. I slip my fingers free so I can touch his skin, heart aching for him as I suddenly realize my family and my problems aren't the only consideration.

"I'm sorry," I whisper into the dark, the rattling of the train almost swallowing my words. But his ear is very close to my lips and he turns to face me, a little frown on his brow.

"I am, too," he says. "I've ruined your life."

I squeeze his hand, leaning my head on his shoulder. "Your parents," I say. "I've been so focused on getting us to California, I forgot you have family."

Sage stiffens, clears his throat. "I don't know what I'd tell them," he says, voice thick. "I guess I should try to call them or something." His thumb traces circles over the back of my hand. "I've thought about it, but I don't know what to say." His free hand runs through his dark hair. "They're used to me rambling around, but this? 'Hi, Mom, Dad, I'm turning into a supernatural creature and could be executed for it?' How do I explain this when I don't truly understand it myself?" Sage's lips brush my forehead. "At least they will still have Zach and Peach." Sage's twin siblings, a boy and girl, half his age. I wish now I'd had a chance to meet his family. He'd offered, several times, but I resisted, knowing we couldn't be. Would it have made things easier for me, if I'd gotten to know them? Or harder?

It doesn't matter now, either way. And this conversation isn't about me, anyway.

"If something happens to me," Sage says.

"You're going to be fine." The words snap out of me, growled in the voice of a wolf.

Sage doesn't say anything for a moment before his body rises and falls in a sigh. "Just, please, tell them something. Make up a story, an accident, something. Don't leave them wondering if I'm alive or dead."

Tears sting my eyes, my mouth tight as I fight off the quiver in my lower lip. "I promise." I won't have to fulfill that promise, so it's easy to make. "Tell me about them?"

He seems surprised. I've never asked before, and, in fact, I've shut him down in the past when he's tried to share. Sage doesn't need further encouragement. I close my eyes and picture his family as he tells me stories about family adventures, like the year they spent in Guatemala volunteering and building schools, his mother's first skydive, his father's passion for snowboarding. They are an incredible family, I can tell from every word he speaks, and his love of them washes over me as I absorb Sage's memories.

"You've been away from them for a long time." I can't remember the last time he went home to visit, though it's possible he didn't tell me because he stopped asking me to join him.

"A year," he says. "I meant to go home for Christmas. Hoped to talk you into coming this time." He laughs, without bitterness. "I guess that's not going to happen, is it?"

I don't comment. I can't. There's nothing to say. I'm silent so long Sage drifts into sleep, breathing regular against my forehead, heartbeat slow and deep. I can't find my own calm, awake with my mind turning for hours, though I'm grateful he manages to get some rest.

I've treated Sage like a toy, at times, a secret love I told no one about. And though I've known all along he has his own feelings, hurts, desires, passions, I've ignored them in favor of my little fantasy. But this is a real life, his is an existence outside my personal experience. And now he's at risk, his whole world, the people who love him about to lose him.

I've been so selfish. As much as I want Sage to be cured, I can't put my desires first. I must find a way to save him and return him to his family, even if that means we are truly done forever.

I wince inwardly. When I chose to let him go before, it was a girl's vanity and pride that drove me. This time, if I get the chance to release him, I will do so out of love, not the call of duty or petulance about my future. I will make sure Sage is safe and happy, without me.

WHERE THE HELL ARE YOU?

I almost leap out of my skin at the shout in my head. I must have dozed off after all, weakening my shields. My heart pounds painfully as I gasp a breath and shove Syd back.

Please, I send as I wall her off, *stay out of this.*

Charlotte. Her words worm their way into my head. *Stubborn, bull-headed, frustrating weregirl! Damn it, let me help you.*

I won't have you put the family in danger for me, I send back, firmly closing the gap. *I won't, Syd. And neither would you in my place.*

She fights me, but I win at last as Sage sits up, eyes wild, but human.

"What's wrong?" He's reaching for his pack while I climb to my feet and take my own, slipping the straps over my shoulders and pulling them tight. The rumbling of the boxcar we're using for transportation makes it hard to hear him, even for my sharp wolf-assisted ears. I head for the partially open door, looking out into the dark. It's been a long night. We've crossed the country once again, it seems, heading for Luhansk far to the east to lay false trail. But now that Syd has found me, we have to disembark and find another route. I wouldn't put it past her to come looking for me and I just can't have that.

I look out into the very late night and hear, to my relief, the engine ahead begins to gear down, the rattling slowing as the train reduces speed. "We must be coming up to a station," I say.

"Luck is with us," Sage says, tightening up the straps on his own bag. He winces as the left strap cuts into his shoulder, but never complains.

"It is," I say. "May it continue so." I feel Syd prod my mind, but she misses more than she hits. Our movement is making it hard for her to pinpoint me.

Which means we need to catch another train, hopefully toward the border. Doing so should shake her off.

"There's a town." Sage leans far out, one hand holding the door. "Not far. We should jump before the train stops."

I nod. "Ready."

We wait another minute until the train is barely moving before we leap out into the brush at the side of the tracks. I crouch there, watching the cars pass, waiting for signs we've been spotted, but nothing happens. Sage is grinning again and I wish he wouldn't. Because I smile back, as though this is fun somehow and not life and death. His life and death.

I lead the way once the train is past, over the metal rails, skirting the back end of the train yard and through a thin copse of trees. A roadway sits on the other side, past a deep ditch filled with brush. My hands reach for Sage as we slip down into it, helping him climb the other side.

He is sweating and cursing softly under his breath when we reach the top. "Sorry," he says through gritted teeth. "I'm holding us back."

He is. But he's the reason we're running, so I won't begrudge him the time it takes. "You're injured," I say, as gently as I can as we shake off the clinging bits of twigs and leaves we brought up with us. "We'll manage."

"I'm just not used to being weak." He bounces his pack on his back, wincing. "This is so frustrating,

Charlotte."

My fingers trace the line of his jaw, compassion tightening my throat. "I know," I say. "I'm sorry, Sage. I wish this hadn't happened to you."

He grasps my hand in his, green eyes intense. "On the other hand," he says, "this is the most time we've spent together ever. And I'm turning into a werewolf. Kind of. Which means maybe we don't have to be over." I just stare at him. He has no idea, even now. I thought he understood. This changes nothing between us. But he looks so determined, do I dare shatter his hope?

I choose not to, turning instead on the road, looking into town. Sage hesitates beside me, but I shrug. "We need food," I say.

His eyes light up. "Starving," he says.

The town is small, but not tiny, big enough to lose ourselves for a few hours. A beat-up hostel sign draws me in and we rent a space in the ancient house. The young man at the desk seems upset to be disturbed at such a late hour, but he grumpily hands us keys anyway before going back to his nap.

Luck again. We don't have to share a room with anyone else, able to take one on our own. But when I try to leave Sage in the tiny space, he resists me.

"I can move around easier on my own," I say. "And you need rest." I point at his shoulder. He's rubbing it absently. As though just noticing, he drops his hand with a wince of guilt.

"I'm fine." He stands and I push him down again.

"I'll be back." I leave him without another word, hoping he'll behave himself. As I step out into the street, hands in my pockets, shoulders hunched against the cold, I wonder if I'm wrong. Maybe I should have brought him with me. But he's not trained to go unnoticed like I am, and if something happens and his wolf appears, he will give us away for certain.

At least this little place offers no danger. I feel no sign of Enforcers or werewolves, no scent to warn they've been here. Just slightly suspicious and watchful early morning townsfolk, like every other small place in Ukraine. It's an hour before dawn, but the sun is late to rise this time of year, and the shops are already opening for business.

Food is easy to procure, a healthy slab of sausage smothered in sauerkraut and two servings of fresh bread, steaming from the oven. I'm salivating over them as I carry the bundle back to the hostel, thinking of my next move.

If the border is being watched, we'll have to find an unguarded place to cross. There are certain areas I know we can make it without dealing with normal authority, though it's possible the Enforcers know about them, too. I'm out of resources to tap, refusing to go back to Iosif for more help. We're on our own, but I have faith I can figure it out.

I have to figure it out. Failing Sage is no option at all.

As a fresh whiff of bread reaches me from the container in my hands, the hostel just ahead, I think of Syd. I've been shoving her away, but we could ask her for help. Not direct, not to have her come to us, but maybe some other assistance? I don't want her involved, not because I don't trust her, but because I love her and the coven. It's comforting knowing I can go to her, though, if things fall apart completely. And she did offer, though she's given up for the moment. But if I can keep her out of this, I will. She might be all-powerful and think no one can harm her, but if she stands against Femke and the werenation, not to mention her own witch Council, she puts her whole coven in danger.

I can't do it. Not after everything she's done for me.

Last resort, then. And only if her help can be taken without putting her family at risk.

The trouble is I know I can get Sage to California eventually. But will we make it in time? Sage might not feel like a real revenant, but there is no doubt he's changing. Seeing his wolf rising proved that to me. And we're already a day and a half out, or more. I have no idea when Sage was bitten, specifically. According to Femke's file, we only have a week at the most.

Five more days, tops. We'll just have to make it

work.

I catch a familiar scent as I climb the stairs, but when I sniff again, all I smell is bread. Still, I come to a halt at the top of the steps, hyper-focused on the world around me. I know that scent, but from where? I almost toss aside the food, the heavy aroma of sausage cutting off my ability to separate smells.

But no, there's nothing. I'm imagining things, fear making me nervous and stressed. And yet, I am careful in the final steps to the door to our room, the bundle of food balanced in one hand as I reach for the knob with my right and draw a deep breath.

Letting it out with an anxious sigh as I step inside.

Sage looks up with a shrug. "Company," he says.

Maksym and Isabelle, my werefriend and the vampire girl he loves, offer little waves as I sag against the door behind me.

FIVE

I don't get a chance to respond. Sage's face alters suddenly, mouth open as he pounces on me and wrenches the food containers from my hand. He sinks to the floor, stuffing sausage and bread into his mouth while I push away from the door and cross my arms over my chest, ignoring the snuffling, grunting sounds from my love as I glare at the pair seated on the bed.

"Don't be angry," Maks says, hands up, distressed. He looks almost comical, his handsome, broad face scrunched like a boy who knows he's done wrong. "Please, Charlotte. We're here to help."

Isabelle nods, rising, leaving the hulking form of her dark-haired boyfriend to come to my side and hug me. I relent, hugging her back, breathing in the hints of rose and oil I always scent from her, mentally kicking myself. The aroma I caught in the hall was so familiar because it was hers mixed with Maks. Despite my slip of security, it's good to see familiar faces, though Maks looks concerned by Sage's behavior, watching him eat with his wolf in his eyes while food disappears in massive bites through Sage's lips. Even Isabelle shudders when she looks down at him.

"He's fine," I snap, bringing their attention back to me. Sage looks up, then down, as though only then realizing what he's doing. He stands with the remains of the food, bashful smile sweet as he offers the mess he left behind to me.

"Sorry," he says.

I shake my head, too anxious to eat now. "Finish it," I say as I turn to the pair who have hunted us down. I'm even more worried than ever, seeing them standing here. "How did you find us?" If they did, we are more vulnerable that I thought.

"We've been searching everywhere for you," Isabelle says, taking a seat again, prim and ladylike beside her muscular wereboyfriend. "When Sydlynn contacted us and told us where she found you, we assumed you would depart the train and find another route. We just lucked out tracking you here."

"Who else did she tell?" I don't mean to be harsh,

and I trust Syd completely, but…

"No one." Maks shakes his head with some violence. "She told us in confidence, warned us on pain of death to be discreet. She wanted to come herself, but she said she would instead find a way to mask your movements against others who search for you."

Bless her. I sag a little in relief. She's found a way to help even if I refuse direct aid from her.

"She suggests we try Wilhelm Castle," Isabelle says. "Sunny will welcome both of you and protect you while we figure out what to do."

"There is nothing to figure out," I say. "If Sage goes back, he's dead. And I won't let that happen."

Isabelle glances at Sage who stares into the remains of the food, mind obviously far away. "He's changed?"

"Just his eyes so far." I shrug. "It was inevitable."

"I'm in the room," Sage says, "in case you've forgotten."

I reach down and stroke his hair. "I know," I say. "I'm sorry."

He stands, setting the empty containers aside, wiping the back of hand over his mouth. "You've been running this show," he says. "Dragging me out of there like I didn't have a choice. Well, I want choices, Charlie."

He doesn't know what he's asking. Or what's good for him.

Isabelle stands and comes to us, touches his hand.

"What do you want to do, Sage?"

He shivers at the contact. Does he sense she's not human? I've told him of vampires, but I don't think he knows she's one.

"Who is this Sunny again?" He turns to me instead of addressing her.

"She is the queen of the Wilhelm family," I say.

Sage blanches. "Oh, yeah. Right. The vampires." He shivers before looking at Isabelle. It's dark in the room, but almost dawn. I know she'll be forced to flee from us soon. "You're one of them?"

She laughs, a tinkling sound, as Maks reacts with a growl to Sage's nervous question.

"I won't hurt you," she says. "Promise."

Sage relaxes visibly, shaking himself. "Sorry," he says. "This is all new to me."

Isabelle nods, brushing off his fear before turning back to me. But her question is for Sage. "Then tell us, what do you want to do?"

Sage rolls his left shoulder. "Will going to the queen put her in danger?"

I don't answer, leaving it to Isabelle.

"Possibly," she says. "But she's willing to take that chance." She smiles at me. "For Charlotte."

Sage's thoughtful expression makes me weak in the knees. "You seem to have a lot of powerful people who love you enough to put their lives on the line to save you."

"And the one I love," I say.

Isabelle nods. "I can't take you now," she says. "It's too close to dawn. But if you two can hide here for the day, we'll be back, with help."

I nod, taking Sage's hand. He seems optimistic about this idea. "We'll see you at dusk," I say.

Isabelle looks relieved, though Maks squints at me, at how easily I've given in. I wave them off as Isabelle flickers into shadow, taking her frowning werewolf lover with her.

The instant they are gone, I lunge for the bed and grab the two backpacks. Sage gapes at me as I shove his into his arms and spin, heading for the door.

"Where are you going?" He stands there, the pack in his hands, mouth open in shock.

"As far from here as we can get," I say. "Before dark falls."

Sage resists. I can smell it on him, my magic feeling his defiance.

"If this queen of theirs can help us," he starts.

"She can do nothing," I say. "She was there when you were first bitten, Sage. She tried, Sebastian tried. Syd's best people tried. And nothing. So running to Wilhelm will only get us cornered and caught. Please." I draw a breath, forcing down my panic. "You have to listen to me. I'm going to save you. But only if you trust me, and only me. I can't fight you every step of the way."

Sage caves, coming to my side. He smells of sausage and bread and the musk of a wolf. When he kisses me, I kiss him back with passion. And when we part, the fire of our embrace between us, he nods.

"Always," he says. "I trust you with my life."

"Then come on," I say, pulling him along behind me. "We have to get out of here."

It's a short hike through town to the other side. We may be forced to hitchhike, though I would prefer to take another train. Anonymity is our best choice at this point.

"We're on our own, then, aren't we?" Sage sounds resigned.

"You knew that," I say, doing my best not to be sharp with him.

"I guess," he says. "It's just sinking in now. We've had so many of your friends try to help, I figured something or someone would come to our rescue." He makes a silly face. "I'm an idiot."

"No," I say, sighing as our feet match pace down the rutted pavement and the chill of the late September wind cuts through our conversation. "Not an idiot. Just optimistic. It's one of the things I love—" I choke off. I can't speak of love and such things right now. I can't afford to lose my focus.

Sage's hand grips mine. "So what's the plan?"

"We stay low," I say, "and out of the reach of the

Enforcers. Syd might be doing her best to distract them from us, but she'll only succeed for so long."

"I still can't believe it," he says, a little laugh in his voice. "Syd Hayle, a powerful witch. I mean, I knew there was something about her when we trained." He runs his right hand through his hair, over the stubble on his cheek and chin with a rasping sound. "I figured she was some kind of special, hiding in plain sight, especially with you watching over her. But I had no idea."

I squeeze his hand. "That's the point," I say. "Normals aren't supposed to."

He shivers. "Normals," he says. "I'm not one anymore, am I?"

Not by a long shot.

I'm distracted from the melancholy of our talk by the faint whistle of a train approaching. "Come on," I say, pulling him along beside me, running toward the sound. "Our ride is calling."

By the time the train chugs past, one of the open cars beckoning, I've shaken off the sadness roused by our chat. But when Sage and I leap onto the rocking platform, landing in unison, I feel it return. He wedges himself carefully between a pair of tarped-over piles of crates, pulling me down next to him. I would have preferred a boxcar with walls, but this will do, especially when he slips his arms around me and cuddles me close.

I have no idea where this run will take us, ultimately.

Or if he'll ever be normal again. But these moments together, when I can almost pretend everything is right in the world and we're just on an adventure, helps me forget for a time, or pretend to, at least.

SIX

I crouch in the tree line on the near side of the
Ukraine border and watch a jeep rumble past. This
section used to be unguarded, the fence easy to climb.
But someone has increased security. If we are to pass
here, we must be very cautious.

Hungary lies on the other side. Perhaps I'd be
smarter to use the Slovenian crossing. But we are here,
now, and I must make a choice.

"Can we do it?" Sage's whisper carries to my ear,
barely a breath of sound. He knows how to keep his
voice down.

"I think so." I sit back on my haunches, looking up
at the sky. It's almost dark again. I want to be over the
border before Isabelle and Maks return. I know my
werefriend will hunt us, though the travel on the train will

hamper his task. Still, if we can reach Hungary, I can steal a car or hitch on another train and cover huge distance before they can figure out where we've gone.

The jeep pauses by the fence, two soldiers emerging with machine guns. One steps behind the vehicle and relieves himself, steam rising from his stream. I chew my lower lip as the second lights a cigarette, calls out a joke in Hungarian I barely understand, my translation skills rusty. His friend laughs. When they step back into the jeep and drive off, I exhale in relief.

Not a border patrol, per se. Just a quick look by a pair of soldiers. Our chances have just improved.

"Stay low," I say, slinking into the tall grass. Sage follows as I slip across the thirty feet to the fence and look around. Nothing, no cameras, no guards and the fence itself isn't electrified. In fact, it's rusting in places, easy enough to make a hole rather than being forced to scale it. With Sage's shoulder the way it is, I'm not sure he could climb.

The wire cutters are cold in my hand as I work on the fence. Sage stares in awe.

"Where did you get those?"

I shrug as the first links part with a soft twang in the dying light. "Stole them in the last town," I say.

Sage's frown hurts me.

"We're on the run," I say. "You wanted me to find a store and buy some?"

He hesitates and shakes his head at last. "Sorry," he says. "You're right. They're just cutters."

He has no idea this is going to be the least of our criminal activities. Though it's odd he cares I stole a pair of wire cutters when he's made no complaint about hitching free rides on train cars. I'll consider his skewed sense of morality later.

I slip through the hole I've made, careful not to catch my pack on the broken links. Sage joins me, deft and as sure as I am in movement. If I'm to run with anyone, he's an excellent choice, at least. If only his issues don't get in the way of our success.

We run toward the trees on the other side of the border, feet pounding a moment over the hard-packed concrete road. The rumble of a jeep engine returning pushes me harder, but we are safely inside the woods before the lights of the vehicle flash behind us. I keep running, exhilarated by the experience, knowing I shouldn't be enjoying myself. But the wolf in me loves this, the chase, even if she's the one being pursued and I can't help but embrace her enthusiasm.

This is how I'm meant to be, the life I'm supposed to live. I've been trained for this, to endure constant threat, the steady pressure of tension, the protective instincts to watch over the one I serve filling me with satisfaction. And no, Sage isn't exactly a bonded client. But it feels the same, in many ways.

How can I ever go back to living in a shining palace with everything done for me? I snort in my head as we run. I may never have to worry about that again, considering what I've done. Death could wait for me on my return. Or imprisonment. So my reticence over being queen of the werenation may be unfounded from here on in.

I shake my head. Oleksander won't let that happen. He'll find a way to stuff me into a coronation dress with a giant crown on my head and chain me to the throne with a weremate and a pack of whining cubs to continue the Moreau family line forever.

I'm grateful when lights sparkle ahead, needing the distraction from the morose image I've created of my future. The next town greets us, the sky now full dark. As we walk its streets to the other side, I realize there is no train station. I ponder our options as we circle around the outlying homes, though my mind is made up for me when the distant sound of a siren goes off, followed by the pressure of Enforcer magic coming closer.

A small house at the far end of town is dark and quiet. Their little car hunches in the driveway, just begging for an adventure of its own. Sage keeps pace with me, though he stops when I test the driver's side door and find it open. I'm already checking for keys when he hisses in my ear, looming in the opening like a thick shadow.

"What are you doing?"

"What does it look like?" I push him back. "Get in, and hurry up about it."

Sage moves slowly, more slowly than I'd like when a flip down of the visor rewards me with a key. It's an old Volvo, clunky and cranky, but the engine fires up the moment I turn the key and, fortunately, the house beside stays dark. If we can just get away before the owners wake...

Sage stands outside the passenger door, immobile once again. I lean sideways, fury firing my muscles, and push the door open. It slams into him before he can catch it.

"Get. In." I show him my wolf. He scrambles to obey as my eyes flare with power, though from the anguished expression on his face, he'd rather be anywhere than here. For that matter, so would I, but he just has to deal with it.

I drive away, moving slowly through the lower gears with the headlights dark, though I want to press the gas to the floor. The shift creaks a bit, but the car responds well and we're soon trundling down the road. I glance back, see the house behind is still cloaked in black and thank the Universe for our good fortune. Sage hugs his bag in the passenger's seat, scowling, looking straight ahead. I punch him lightly on the shoulder, only then remembering his wound and wincing as he flinches from the blow.

"Don't shut me out," I say. "Or judge me, Sage. Nothing matters to me, nothing but keeping you alive. And I will murder, steal and fight to the death to make sure you are okay. Is that understood?"

He doesn't respond at first, still rigid. I snap my teeth together at him, my wolf's irritation showing while I finally turn on the headlights and push down on the gas pedal.

"Fine," I say. "But I'll drag you, kicking and screaming, if I have to. Mark my words."

Sage exhales heavily and nods. "Thank you," he says, voice quiet. "But I can't help it, Charlotte. I'm not this kind of person."

And I am? Yes, I am. What does that make me to him? And mean for us?

He reaches out, takes my hand. "Don't think I'm not grateful," he says. "And I have no idea what kind of horrible life you've led that this is normal for you. Or possible."

I wish I could shake off the pity in his voice. I don't need or want it. "Be happy I'm who I am," I say. "Or you'd be dead already."

"I'm very grateful," he says, sitting back head turned to the passenger window. "But I wish it was different."

He's quiet a long time and I hold my peace, fighting for calm. This could turn into a fight, and we don't have time to argue. The last thing I need is to battle Sage every step when I'm just trying to save him.

Sage finally turns back to me, cheeks pink in the light of the dash. "So we're in Hungary," he says. His entire tone, being, scent, everything tells me he doesn't want to fight, either. I relax a little and nod.

"We have papers and money," I say. "We should be fine if we don't draw the attention of the Enforcers." And the hunting werewolves. I know Caine must be still seeking us, too. "We'll ditch this car in a few hours and find another train to take us to Switzerland." I add another layer of muffling to the shields I've built, the reminder all I need to add to our magic protections. It feels odd to suppress my power. I spent so many years out of control, when I was still a slave of the Black Souls. Syd's gift has been incredible, but this trip down memory lane makes me nervous.

"Charlie," Sage says, voice soft and careful. "I barely know anything about you, and I'm only just now realizing it."

Why does he have to bring this up? "Not much to tell," I say, hoping my gruff tone will shut him down.

No such luck. Sage is relentless when he wants something, though, as usual, he's gentle about it. "Your grandfather," he says, "the king. He wasn't always a king, was he?"

How does he know anything? I told him a bit when

I explained his situation, but nothing of our past as a werenation.

"It doesn't matter," I say.

"It does to me." Sage's hands tighten on the straps of his bag, still perched in his lap as though he's ready to run at any second, moving car or not. "A lot."

Sage's jaw tightens. I catch his stubborn reaction out of the corner of my eye and scowl right back. "When you're safe," I say, doing my best to keep my mind from exploring my past on its own. "We'll talk and I'll tell you what I can."

He draws a breath and I know he's going to argue. We're going to fight after all. But no. He turns away again.

"Fine," he says. "I'm holding you to that."

We drive on into the quiet darkness while I dread that distant conversation and vow to find a way to hide everything I've been through from him if it's the last thing I do.

SEVEN

I pull over in a small town for gas, and at a late-night deli for food. There is no hostel, and I'm just as glad. Stopping right now will only put us in unnecessary danger.

We park in an abandoned farmyard to eat and have a quick rest, the hulking, empty house shadowing us from sight. Sage devours his food as quickly as he had before, though he seems more aware and less savage about it. I allow a few hours to close my eyes in the shelter of the empty home and crumbling outbuildings. We probably shouldn't stop, but I have to catch rest when I can. I can't burn out until I've found what I'm looking for.

A solid five hours of sleep does me a world of good, though I shudder at the black holes of the home's dark windows, feeling as though it's watching us, waiting to see what we'll do. Abandoned places have always given me the creeps, reminding me of years of loneliness I'll never get back.

Sage wakes when I do, finishing the last of my half-eaten meal as I fire up the engine and drive off again. I think about his demand, his desire to know of my past, what made me as I am. And shudder from ever telling him. How could he possibly understand the things I was forced to endure, to do, to survive my youth and young adulthood at the hands of the Dumonts? He would never be able to cope. Never. Then again, am I not giving him enough credit? He loves me for who I am. Still loves me now, though I've led him to the brink of his death, to danger and life as a fugitive. It's possible Sage would simply accept and I could finally talk to someone about the past without fear.

Maybe someday. Maybe. For now, he loves me, yes. But he's with me because he has to be. Because without me, he'd be dead. I can't trust I'm his first choice until this is all over and he's healed. If he still wants me, isn't pressured into a life with me, perhaps then I'll consider it. But in this time and place, telling him won't solve anything, and could drive him away.

If I were him, I wouldn't be anywhere near me, knowing what I know about what I've done.

Dawn breaks lovely over the eastern horizon. Morning finds us nearing the Austrian border and I finally relent when Sage looks longingly out the window at a town appearing in the distance. We need to get out and stretch our legs anyway, and we've come so far so quickly I'm fairly confident we're safe for the moment.

The little border town is just outside Sopron, a small collection of stone-built homes and little shops on a picturesque main street. Sage steps out and immediately turns on his heel, a grin on his face. He hasn't smiled or spoken much since last night's conversation, so I find his sudden enthusiasm encouraging.

"I smell meat." He drifts toward the door of a deli and I follow him, eyes scanning the street. I really need to dump this car as soon as possible. It's morning, and the owners will certainly have it declared stolen by now.

I'm slow to follow Sage inside, but when I hear his growl, I run for the half-open door. The butcher stands behind the counter, face white as old ash, hands trembling around his cleaver as Sage leans over the counter, trying to grab the raw meat on the slab.

I have to risk using power, slamming it into Sage to knock him back. He spins on me, eyes a wolf's, hands curving into claws, though not fully transformed. I pin him with magic, mind locking on his.

ENOUGH. I'm his dominant and his wolf knows it. It retreats while Sage staggers, hand pressing to his forehead where beads of sweat stand out. The butcher stares at us while I struggle with what to do, what to say.

"Sorry," I offer with a weak smile. "He's a bit of an animal when he's hungry."

Oh, Charlotte.

The butcher tries to smile, licking his lips nervously as my magic encourages him to forget what he saw, chalk it up to his imagination. My wolf whispers to him while my heart pounds with worry. All this power use is going to draw attention.

We have to get out of here.

I lead Sage toward the door as the butcher relaxes, shrugs and goes back to work, though still shaken. Sage fights me when I drag him out onto the street, shaking him a little.

"Pull it together," I snarl in his ear.

"Starving," he pants back at me.

"I know." I feel his hunger, the blood lust of his rising wolf. "I'll find you something. But we have to go now."

Sage whimpers, but returns to himself. "Sorry," he says. "Charlie, I'm so sorry."

I shake my head, leading him to the car. "It's not your fault," I say, in pain for him. "This is my fault."

"Funny," a familiar voice says, "you're not the only one blaming yourself for this mess."

I look up with a gasp to find my sorcerer friend—and one time mate possibility—Piers Southway, leaning casually against the bonnet of our stolen car with his arms crossed over his chest. His gray longcoat is dusty at the hem and he has a bruise on one high cheekbone. But his grin is as jaunty as ever, if tight with bitterness, shining blond hair hanging over one narrow shoulder.

"Piers." I breathe his name, panic rising all over again. "Please, you have to let us go."

He stands, arms falling to his sides. A hint of sadness flickers across his face before he comes to my side, touches my cheek. Sage growls at him, but Piers ignores the threat.

"I'm here to help," he says.

"I used magic." I tug Sage toward the car. "The Enforcers will track it."

"They would," Piers says with a grin, "if I didn't get here first and use sorcery to block it."

I could kiss him, right there in the street, but Sage is between us, glaring at Piers. I know it's not him, it's the wolf rising in him, but it's enough of a distraction to hold me back.

"Thank you," I say. And hesitate. "You want us to go to Austria?" The border is a short skip away, though Castle Wilhelm is not on my list of tourist stops.

Piers shakes his head, opening the passenger door for me. "The vampire plan was a terrible one," he says. "They will know you're with Sunny the moment you set foot at Wilhelm."

Leave it to Piers to agree with me. "Then what?"

I'm used to working on my own, but having him here makes me feel better. Guilt over that when I'm still holding Sage in my arms makes my heart ache.

"Dunno," Piers says. "Though I've always wanted to be a fugitive."

I gape at him. "You're not coming with us."

Piers's grin is tight, angry. "Yes," he says. "I am. I can't transport you directly—my mother is watching my power output. She'll know if I move more than me. But I can come with you and make sure you have backup if you need it."

His presence is going to make things more complicated, but only with Sage. My love snaps and snarls from the front seat as I push him into the cushion. "We have to find another car," I say, grateful for Piers as he firmly closes the door.

"Simplicity itself." He touches the roof and the entire shape twists, transforms. Colors shift from dirty yellow to deep green. I circle to check the plate, watch it change as well. "Now," Piers says, reaching for the driver's door. "Are you coming or not?"

EIGHT

Piers's capable hands grip the wheel as he drives toward the border. I perch behind him and Sage, wedging myself between the front seats. Sage has calmed somewhat, but his hostility for Piers wafts toward me like a flower's aroma and I know having my sorcerer friend here is triggering the wolf in Sage far more than anything else has.

There is only one explanation. My love's wolf feels Piers's affection for me and sees him as a threat. But I can't bring myself to ask Piers to leave.

"So," the handsome young Southway says in his cheerful voices, "where are we heading besides Austria?"

"California," I say. He glances sideways at me, a little surprised.

"Why California? Ah!" He answers his own question

before I can respond. "Caine and his pack."

"They are revenants, I'm sure of it." I lower my head, mind whirling. "But they are different, Piers. Controlled, somehow. And they must have access to power, because they haven't devolved into emptiness and insanity."

"Controlled," he says. "Like your people were when the Black Souls created them," Piers nods. "You think sorcerers have been trying to make new werewolves." He shrugs at my tilted head. "I caught most of that when you were talking to Syd. So you think the answer to Sage's problem," as though it's just a minor inconvenience or something, "resides in California."

"Caine bit him." I know it in my heart. Piers shoots me another look, but doesn't argue or ask for proof while Sage hisses. "Caine's from California. And Sage is nothing like the revenants I've had dealings with. He's totally different, even from Caine and his pack."

"How different?" Piers pulls to a halt behind a thin line of cars. We've reached the border. I'm nervous suddenly, digging for our passports, handing them to my sorcerer friend while I wait for Enforcers to swoop in and take us at any moment. But Piers shows no sign of worry so I can only believe we aren't at risk.

"He feels more like a real werewolf." It's the first time I've said it out loud. I catch Sage's narrowed stare.

"I hate to keep reminding you," he says, voice

mellow despite his glare, "but I am present and accounted for. You really need to stop talking about me like I'm not."

I reach forward and take his hand in mine. He relaxes instantly, though I catch the glance Piers gives our connection and worry about how he's feeling. If it's hurting him, he doesn't show it.

"So you think Sage is a successful revenant, whatever these sorcerers were trying to achieve." We move forward one car length.

"I do," I say. "Which means they will be looking for him," I meet Sage's eyes, "for us, too, won't they?" Another truth I haven't allowed myself to speak until now.

Piers nods abruptly. "Good thing I'm with you after all," he says. He shakes the steering wheel with a surge of anger. "Damn it, if only I could just take you directly there. But Femke's requested my mother and the Steam Union be on the search for you, too. I know Mum is keeping a close eye on me."

"You being here could put us at risk." Sage has never sounded so empty.

I squeeze his hand again, this time in denial while Piers sighs.

"Possibly," he says, pulling up at last to the border station with our passports in one hand and a smile on his face for the agent. "But until that's proven to me, I'm not going anywhere but with you two."

I wait for the guard to have us arrested, certain Iosif has failed me, that this is some grand scheme to capture Sage again. But when the smiling guard hands the passports back and Piers drives off into Austria, I finally allow myself to release the anxiety keeping my body tense.

"We need to reach a major center," Piers says. "And fly to the States."

I nod. "But far from Ukraine," I say. "How far?"

Piers releases one hand from the steering wheel and runs it over his blond ponytail, the end of it brushing over my free hand. The silk strands tickle.

"I'm thinking we're tourists," he says, bright and vapid. "Seeing Spain for the first time. But we need to get home for school, don't we?" His British accent vanishes as he turns to Sage. "Right, bro?"

Sage frowns. "I'm not your bro."

I poke my love and wink, schooling my own accent to General American. "It's been fun and all," I say, "but yeah. Time to go home to the good old US of A."

Piers laughs. "Perfect."

We're barely ten miles from the border when I feel them. I've only just sat back to try to close my eyes for a while, when the pressure of Enforcer magic wakes me and drives me forward in my seat.

Piers hisses and nods without speaking. He's felt them, too. We pull over abruptly, Piers slamming open the driver's door while I scramble out the back, helping Sage with our bags as Piers gestures for us to hurry.

We slip into the woods on the steep road and run for cover. I glance back, see the car revert to the state we'd stolen it in, knowing that will alert the Enforcers they are on our trail. Lights in the distance pull us forward, to civilization in the form of another small town.

"We need a new ride." Piers leaves me with Sage who pants like a dog. Not out of breath, but from intensity and worry. I grip his hand tightly, not daring to risk a touch of power to help him pull himself down from the brink of his wolf. He's recovered enough when Piers pulls up a moment later in a shiny red sports car.

"Get in."

I don't care where it's come from, or if it still looks like the one Piers actually stole. All I care about is Sage and escape. The touch of the Enforcers is still there, but focused on something, most likely the car we abandoned. I slip into the back, the tiny space barely big enough for Sage, let alone the two of us, and hold on as Piers hits the gas and peels away.

"They must have tracked the car," Piers says, tension in his voice. "We should be okay, now."

I'm perched in Sage's lap, the bags squished beside us, my head pressed to the roof. He's hot, his temperature running higher than normal, and he lets out a sharp hiss when I try to adjust my position. I brush my lips over his cheek as an apology, resisting the sudden urge to kiss him, if only to spare Piers the sight of us making out in the back seat while he drives us to safety.

I settle as best I can, flexing muscles when my foot tries to go to sleep. It's not long before I feel them again, the Enforcers. They might not have our scent, but they know we are close and they are gaining on us.

Piers swears in three different languages before pulling over in another town. Some kind of festival is happening, streamers and balloons everywhere. We abandon the car in the back of a petrol station and hurry into the morning's crowd of celebrants.

"Now what?" Sage's voice is a deep growl.

"We keep running," Piers says. "I just need to get us away from here."

The mass of people must do the trick, because the press of Enforcer magic bypasses us and moves on. I pull on Sage, tugging him after Piers, and, within a few minutes, we're driving again, this time in a small family van my sorcerer friend has liberated.

"Made the mistake of using sorcery to disguise the car last time," he says as I drive after taking the keys from his hands. "This should do it."

Sage is in the back with our bags, leaning forward between the seats as I'd done. "Or," he says in cold monotone, "you being with us is attracting them."

I don't want to believe it, but Sage might be right.

"You said your mother would know," I say.

"She can't be watching me that carefully." The denial in Piers's voice turns to regret. "Damn her, she's treating me like a lure." He reaches for the wheel, jerks it hard to the side of the road. I slam on the brakes, pull over even as he opens the door, ready to leap out though the van is only just coming to a stop. "I'm sorry," he says. "I thought I was helping. Be safe, get to an airport." He takes the scarf from around my neck. Pauses and kisses me abruptly. Sage snarls, but Piers is already moving again, leaning in the back to liberate one of Sage's gloves. "I'll lead them away, make them think you're with me. Should give you time to get away. Dump this van, get on a train. The speed will confuse them if I fail." Piers pauses one moment, anguish showing. "I'll see you in California."

He slams the door, waving me on. I glance back, seeing his tall body retreat in the rearview just before a tunnel of black opens.

Charlotte, he sends. *Maybe I was wrong about Wilhelm.*

And then, he's gone.

NINE

Sage isn't happy about the kiss, I can tell, but I ignore him as we pull into the next town and hunt down a train station. It's easy enough to find. And this time, I go to the ticket booth and buy tickets.

The smiling attendant gestures at the map before me. "Where to?" Her Austrian is crisp and aristocratic.

I answer in English, my American accent firmly in place. "Spain," I say.

"By way of Wilhelm," Sage cuts in. I glare at him but he shakes his head. "You promised we could see it before we went home, remember?"

I'll kill him later. The attendant hands over the tickets after I pay her. "Have a pleasant trip," she says in heavily accented English.

We board with the other passengers, the two seats

across from us empty when the train pulls out of the station. I toss our bags across, putting my feet up, staring out the window.

"Don't be mad," Sage says. "But if your friend has doubts, maybe we should talk to the vampires before we go to California."

I turn to scowl at him. "I told you," I said. "This is a bad idea. It will only mean trouble for everyone."

"Maybe," he says. "Maybe not. Remember, that Sebastian guy wanted to try to make me a vampire." I'm startled by his words. "Maks and Isabelle told me," he said, "while we were waiting for you." He shivers a little, but smiles. "Not that I'm all that eager to be a vampire or anything, but if it saves us from having to go further, I'm for it. Especially if it keeps me from turning into a monster."

I take his hand and squeeze it. Maybe he's right. But I can only feel growing nervousness at the idea, and my intuition tells me this is a terrible idea.

"Fine," I say. "We'll give it a try. But if it fails…" I have no reason to believe it would, though. Vampires come from normals, just like werewolves had in the beginning.

"If it fails," Sage says, "we go to California and see what we can find out."

We hold hands the whole trip, though I rise once to go to the washroom. I stare at my drawn and anxious face in the mirror, gaze going to my blonde hair. I'm going to have to do something about the color before too long. I shake myself. Here I am, planning for the worst. But that's me, isn't it? It's what's kept me alive for so long. I'd almost forgotten my old training, but here it is, coming back to save me.

Sunny and Sebastian won't be able to help. I have to have a plan.

It's only a few hours more when the train pulls into the station near Wilhelm. Sage and I disembark, he with eagerness, me with hesitation. It's only a few miles to Castle Wilhelm from Wolfsburg. I try not to dwell on the irony of the name.

Sage scowls unhappily at me when I pull up to the platform where I've left him. He eyes the stolen motorcycle. I don't give him a chance to argue, tossing him a helmet. The big machine responds to me as I drive, pushing the speed to the limit. The winding roads are no challenge to my werewolf reflexes and I feel myself relax into the focus of controlling the heavy bike through the dangerous turns.

Castle Wilhelm is well hidden, though the entire area is named for the vampire family. I wonder if normals realize where the title comes from or that the castle itself even still exists. I have no trouble finding the turnoff, magically shielded, because I know the entrance as though born to it. I'm forced to slow, the gravel road almost impossible for the powerful motorcycle to navigate at speed. By the time we come to a purring halt at the gates to the castle, the sun has gone down again.

The third day is half over and we're no closer to saving Sage. Or are we? It's possible my cynicism will prove unwarranted. But when I dismount and head for the gate, Sage behind me, struggling with both backpacks, I know in my heart this is far from over.

I stagger at the touch of Enforcer magic. They are here, waiting for us! I'm a fool, I've walked right into a trap. But as I spin back to sprint to Sage, mouth open to warn him, two figures shudder from shadow, barely solidifying. One engulfs Sage before vanishing, the other embracing me.

"You're safe," Isabelle's voice whispers to me before I'm drowned in her power.

Only a heartbeat later, I step out of the shivering shadows and onto the red carpet leading to Sunny's throne. The queen of the Wilhelm vampire clan rushes toward me, her husband, Frank, releasing Sage and stepping back, our second rescuer.

Sunny hugs me tight, her physical coldness a clear sign she hasn't even found time to eat. When she leans back, her face is dark with purpose.

"Come," she says, holding her hand out to Sage as the feeling of the Enforcers grows closer, "we must hurry."

He takes her offered fingers and we're traveling again, this time with only Sunny. I'm about to ask her to carry us to California when we land in another throne room, this one done in blue and silver.

Sebastian waits for us, wasting no time coming forward to take Sage from Sunny. He stares into my love's eyes while my heart begs me to speak up.

"Would you be a vampire?" Sebastian is no ordinary blood drinker, not any longer. Syd's maji power has made him much more, able to walk in daylight, no longer requiring blood for sustenance. And a heartbeat. But he might not be able to offer Sage what he has, considering his own clan are all still in full thrall of the spirit power animating them, despite his attempts to change them. "I must have your permission to try."

Sage glances sideways at me, panic on his face. I want to tell him to say no, this is wrong. The old prejudices between werewolves and vampires are gone, the taint of Black Soul sorcery no longer keeping us apart. But the wolf in me knows this is wrong and can only lead to more problems.

When I don't say anything, Sage turns back to Sebastian. "Do it," he says.

The Enforcers are coming. I can feel them all over again, this time with purpose. Sunny swears under her breath, turns to me, obviously as aware as I am.

"I should have killed him long ago," she snarls and I

remember her traitor vampire, Piotr Wilhelm. She thinks he's alerted the authorities, and I believe she is right. "Sebastian," she spins on the other vampire leader, "if you're going to do this, make it now."

Rainbow light rises from Sebastian while Sage stares, open mouthed and stunned by the view. I reach for him with my magic, knowing it doesn't matter anymore if the Enforcers feel me. I need to support him if I can. But the power Sebastian controls rejects me, pushes me back, and Sage is left to face this transformation alone.

I cling to Sunny, half of me praying this works if it means saving Sage. And half of me hoping it fails. I want him to be a werewolf. Or human, normal. Am I that prejudiced to think I would no longer feel the same for him, were he a vampire? It will change things. He will live far longer than me, tied to the house DeWinter. And while Isabelle and Maks have found a way to make it work, vampires can't procreate. He will never age, never die. And I will wither away.

Selfish. But true. And at the core of me I finally admit I want him to be a werewolf, if that is possible, to heal him and make him one of us. So we can be together. But I'm lying to myself if I believe that will ever happen, just like he's delusional. I know better. He is a revenant and the best I can hope for is he won't lose his mind. He will never be a true werewolf. Better to find a cure and return him to human, if I can. But I can't let the whispering hope of the girl inside me go.

Enforcer power beats against the wards Sebastian has set around his castle, shaking me from my self-revelation. The shields hold, but they won't last forever. I steel myself against the fact this is about Sage and silence the weeping child who begs for him.

The rainbow light descends over Sage, hugs him close. I hear his heartbeat speed up even more, the sizzle of the touch of his skin on the power, as though he's too hot to be contained. Sage howls, his wolf rising in his eyes, curving his hands into claws while the magic of Sebastian's bloodline tries to break through and make him a vampire.

I feel it fail, know he's safe, and choke on a sob, hating there is relief in the sound. Sunny curses, unladylike for her, and hugs me tighter.

"I'm sorry," she whispers, though I'm not.

Sage staggers to his knees as Sebastian lets him go. Liquid oozes aggressively through the bandages to soak Sage's left shoulder.

"The infection resists me," Sebastian pants, shaking his head. "I can't help him."

Enforcer magic hits hard, shaking the castle. *IN THE NAME OF ALL MAGICKS*, a voice booms in my head. *RELEASE THE FUGITIVES*.

"We have to call Syd." Sunny is reaching for her already, but I cut her off.

"No," I say. "Bad enough I'm attracting trouble for my friends. I won't have any of you involved from this point."

Sebastian stands there, power swirling around him, handsome face grim. "Tell me what you want me to do," he says. "I will go to war for you, Charlotte."

I believe him, but I can't let him. I rush to Sage and cradle him against me. "Just get us out of here," I say as the wards crumble.

Sunny joins us as flares of blue light appear overhead. I look up, see Andre Dumont's angry face, a line of furious Enforcers behind him, as shadows flicker and carry us away.

Sebastian. I send his name to Sunny in a gasp.

He'll be fine, she sends just as we are deposited back in her castle. I recognize this room, where Syd and I stayed while she was on trial. "He can handle them," she says out loud. "But what are the Dumonts doing there?"

I had no idea, and didn't want to know.

"I'll be back," she says, stepping away, already surrounded in shadow. "We'll make this work."

I wait for her to vanish before tugging on Sage. "We have to go."

He nods, groggy, but with me. "This was a terrible idea." He manages a little smile. "When will I learn to listen to you?"

I kiss his cheek, helping him to his feet, already

feeling the Enforcers coming. "I don't know," I say. "But hell will surely freeze over."

"Now what?" He's pale and sweating, but he's aware and beside me and that's all that matters.

"We run," I say. "And go back to plan A."

"California." He hobbles next to me, growing in strength, until we reach the door. I feel Sunny let the Enforcers in even as I slam up my shields around Sage and me.

"You got it, dude." My American accent feels clunky. I'm out of practice.

Sage laughs. "No one says dude anymore."

I roll my eyes as we slip down the corridor. I know exactly where the exits are, found them all in case I had to get Syd out. And the one I need is very close. "Everyone's a critic."

"Your friends." We pause by a tapestry. I pull it aside revealing the door to the exterior.

"Will be fine," I say. "And no matter their intent, the law is the law. They will be forced to turn us over eventually."

"Fugitives it is," Sage says, taking his bag from me, though I know he's still weak. "After you, princess."

The dark night engulfs us and I actually feel better.

TEN

The forest is dark and quiet, the mountain cold. It's grown colder still since the sun went down, a fact I barely noticed on the motorcycle ride, thanks to adrenaline giving me extra heat, and the press of Sage's overheated body against mine. Now my breath puffs in patches of mist before me as Sage and I creep through the Austrian night away from Castle Wilhelm and the searching witches ordered to bring us in.

The Enforcers will have set up a ward around the castle property by now. I'll need to find a way through it if we are to escape. The moment we touch it, try to breach it, they will be on us. If they don't spot us before then. A blue glowing shape drifts overhead, the trees keeping us safe for now. But I have no illusions. They don't need ordinary vision to find us.

I have to keep my magic contained. Which means we have only our feet and our wits to carry us away from here.

A black tunnel appears just beyond the next copse of trees, triggering a wave of blue light. I grimace, but am grateful for the warning. Whoever made that tunnel just found the wards for me.

Piers emerges, cursing, waving us forward. Sage doesn't resist, running with me as flares of blue fire appear in the air overhead, joining the first. I feel witch magic brush over us, deflected for the moment by my shields, but they will break through them when they pinpoint us. We have to escape, and the only way to do that, at the moment, is with Piers.

We dive for the tunnel, Piers behind us, at the exact moment the Enforcer's power locks on me. The black absorbs the magic the Enforcers throw at us, propelling us forward with great speed.

I tumble out the other end, feeling warmer, the air not so crisp, into soft grass. Sage looks up at Piers as I roll out of my crouch and face my sorcerer friend. He seems panicked, hands shaking.

"Run," he says, desperation in his voice. "I've taken you as far as I can. But they'll be coming. I'm sorry. She's betrayed me to them, and I can't help you." I watch him vanish into fresh blackness, knowing he speaks of his own mother.

No time to think about it, to worry about him, only enough to let my heart swell in gratitude a moment while I gather myself for action. I turn and flee as he bid me, Sage at my side, now seemingly fully recovered from what Sebastian's attempt to turn him did. The landscape has changed, the temperature not the only difference and as we run past a storefront in what feels like a city, the sign in French.

"France," Sage says at the same time. "He got us farther."

"As long as the Enforcers don't know it," I say. "We have to go."

We hurry along the street, my eyes scanning for a vehicle we can steal easily and quietly. Sage keeps pace, head down, though I feel his emotions churning.

I finally force us to pause out of the touch of a streetlight, in darkness. There's been no hint of the Enforcers though easily a half hour has passed. Could Piers have figured out a way to keep them from finding us? I can only hope. Maybe he still has our things in his possession. I send him a mental thank you for taking the heat for me.

A little park beckons. I just need a moment to sit and catch my breath, to think things through. Sage sits next to me on a bench of stone under a smiling angel statue with her welcoming arms outspread. The night air is lovely, the clear sky full of stars.

"You love him." Sage's statement comes from nowhere, though when I turn to him, to the hard lines his face has settled into, I realize he's been thinking about this for a long time.

"No," I say. "I don't." I take Sage's hand. "I love you."

He doesn't look at me. "He loves you, though."

I sigh. "Piers is in love with the idea of love." I squeeze Sage's hand. "And my grandfather once thought he would be a good match for me. To save me from having to mate with a werewolf."

"Are they so bad?" Sage's flat tone hurts me.

"No," I say. "But my race isn't known for its cleverness, its kindness. My family is a rarity and even we have our rough edges. And with the pressures of being a princess, of creating a healthy and powerful offspring to be my heir…the last thing I want is a heavy-handed and duty-bound weremate who only has heart for the throne."

Sage is quiet a moment, the stiffness leaving him. "So Piers was your other option."

I nod. "I thought so," I say. "At least he's funny and handsome. I think I could have learned to love him, maybe. Given time. But that's off the table now." It feels odd to have this conversation with him, though he's no longer angry.

"Your grandfather will make you marry a werewolf," Sage says.

"How wise you are." I force a smile. "Yes, exactly. This mess will ensure I am bound to a were, to dispel my dishonor and return dignity to the name Moreau."

Sage looks up at the stars, sad. "I came to find you because I couldn't bear to let you go." He shivers in the faint breeze, though it's not cold here in the south. "I thought I could find a way to convince you. To make you love me enough."

"That was never the question," I say, my own sorrow making its way forward.

"I know that now." He smiles at me as he turns to meet my eyes. "But, I don't regret a thing, Charlotte. Not a bit of it. I'd have spent my life wondering, wishing, pining for you, if I'd let you just walk out of my life like that. The best thing that ever happened to me, and you up and left." He chuckles, shakes his head, dark hair glossy in the streetlight. "I thought I knew the worst that could happen. I figured it would be you saying 'no'."

There's not much I can say to that.

"Does Piers know it's over between you?" He speaks so carefully, his ego wanting to know. It makes me sigh, but not unhappily.

"Don't worry about Piers," I say. "This kind of thing isn't new to him. He used to want Syd, too, you know."

Sage relaxes a little. "She'd eat him for breakfast."

I laugh. It feels good. "And me?"

Sage grins, weak and shaking. "He wouldn't even make it to the orange juice."

I kiss his cheek, laying my head on his right shoulder. Sage slips his arm around me, the scent of him even more wolf than ever, though he remains clean, beautiful, like a fresh morning, not a hint of revenant stench about him.

"I'm sorry," he says. "I didn't mean to be cruel to him. It's this thing inside me." He pats his chest with his left hand, wincing. "It wants to protect you even though you don't need it."

"I might not need it," I say, "but it's nice to know you care."

"I love you, too," he says, fierce in that moment, intense and powerful. "And I won't let anyone hurt you ever again, Charlotte."

If only he had that power. "We have to go." I lean away, only to have my face captured in his hand, my lips covered in his mouth. I lean into his kiss, the fire there burning between us. Sage is my life. This is all worth it.

But when I open my eyes and see the fear in his, I want to cry. I hug him, careful of his damaged shoulder, tears prickling, throat thick. "This is all my fault," I whisper into his hair. "I should never have allowed us to be. I knew the risks, that you could find out what I am, that you would be exposed to infection if I ever bit you as a werewolf."

"You never would," he says.

"Not on purpose." I lean back, wiping my nose on the cuff of my jacket. "But it's part of the reason we rarely mate with normals, Sage. It's just too risky." I pat his leg. "This is my responsibility and I have to take care of it." I meet his eyes, expecting more fear, but seeing only love. "I'm sorry I got you into this."

Sage kisses me again, soft and kind. "Charlotte," he whispers into my mouth. "I wouldn't change a thing, even if it means I have to die."

I do sob then, unable to stop. And when he hugs me, I let him hold me as the moon sets on the third day.

ELEVEN

We find a train station and spend the rest of the night there after buying new tickets. I worry the passports we're using might be compromised, but decide to forget my fear. The Enforcers don't think like normals and would never consider checking for something as ordinary as paperwork. At least, I don't think so. Femke is smart, and far from backward. But when we board without issue and the train leaves for Barcelona, I relax and allow my trust to surface, if only for now.

We step off at the Spanish border long enough to rent a cheap room in a small motel. I purchase hair dye, blackening my blonde locks. When I hack it off at the nape of my neck, Sage sighs his disappointment from where he watches me with sad eyes.

"I love your hair," he says.

I shrug, grinning. "It's been too long," I say, turning to face him dressed only in a towel. "I've been Sharlotta for years now. Time for Charlotte to come out to play." I approach him, running my fingers through his dark hair. "How do you feel about bleach?"

By the time we're done, our roles are reversed, and my darling Sage is a pale blond. I swing my new black bob with confidence, changed into a touristy sundress, him in casual shorts and a T-shirt. I've even replaced our backpacks with rolling bags, to complete the traveler's look.

Our border crossing is simplicity itself and we board the next train for Barcelona. I'm finally feeling like things are going the way they need to. If only they stay that way.

The train drops us close to the airport and a quick taxi ride delivers us to the American Airlines terminal. Sage is acting nervous, but a quick prod and he settles.

"The last thing we need," I whisper to him as we stand in line at the ticket counter, "is for some normal in a uniform to think you're squirrely."

He nods. "Sorry," he says, rotating his left shoulder. I bandaged it back at the hotel, to stop the seeping. But it's still causing him pain. "I know better."

The ticket agent doesn't blink when we ask for two fares to Los Angeles via Miami. She just smiles and hands us the boarding passes after the credit card Iosif gave me approves the purchase.

"Happy flying," she says in her false, perky voice.

I lead Sage with me, our bags small enough to carry on. The terminal is huge, but could be any international departure site. I've been in so many, they are a blur of long corridors and pedways and expensive shops lining the way to multiple gateways around the world.

Still, this airport gives me a feeling of excitement. A few hours from now and we'll be in America. And only a few more after that, California and hopefully the answers we need to save Sage.

We're almost to our gate when I feel it. The touch of Enforcer power. I pour on the shielding, pulling Sage aside, scanning the seating areas for signs of witches. But whomever Femke has put on post to guard the airport feels bored and distracted.

"What?" Sage's grip on my hand tightens.

I smile up at him, shake my head. "Just act normal," I say. "We're almost home free."

As we pass the two young men I've identified as Enforcers, neither even looks up from the conversation they're having. The professional in me is highly irritated. If I ever get a chance to tell her, I know Femke will be very disappointed in their performance.

The seats in coach aren't ideal, but I don't want to risk drawing attention to us by sitting in first class. Sage doesn't complain, taking the window seat. I settle next to him in the center, hoping the aisle remains empty. I don't feel like being forced to have a conversation with a stranger.

Twenty minutes later, the seat beside me is still vacant as the airplane taxis toward the strip. More luck, I'll take it. But as the seatbelt digs in when the pilot turns us onto the runway, I have a horrible thought. Is this too easy? But no, I've done everything right, as I've been trained to do. We're safe and heading where we need to go. Still, the niggling doubt remains. Surely, Femke would know we'd be trying to travel using normal channels. I shift in my seat, uncomfortable suddenly with the knowledge Sage and I are now trapped in a giant prison if the Enforcers choose to come after us.

I force myself to calm down when the plane lifts off, my ears popping from the sudden change in air pressure. They won't risk normals. And if they are waiting on the other end in Miami, so be it. I'll find a way to free us. But they won't try to take us from a plane full of normals.

They won't.

The sound of soft snoring finally shakes me free of my fear. I turn toward Sage to find him sleeping with his head against the bulkhead, hands curved in his lap. I lean in and kiss his cheek, knowing he's the smart one. I need to get some sleep of my own. I've been up and running for days now, the few hours of rest here and there hardly enough. But someone has to watch over him.

The flight attendant smiles as she offers me a drink and a snack. I pick at my peanuts, sip my water, the moments passing adding to my relief and the niggling doubt in equal measure. Maybe I'm just too good at this to ever really believe I've done what I need to do to win our freedom.

As I set aside my snack, I catch a whiff of a hot meal being served up front in first class. We're only two rows back from the curtain dividing the haves from the cattle. It's chicken of some kind, smells delicious.

It's not until Sage stirs beside me I realize how much danger we're in. I look up and into the gaze of a wolf, sharp canines glowing as he snarls his hunger. Damn it, why didn't I feed him before we got on the plane? I know better. But I was distracted, in a hurry, thinking only of escape. It's not like me to miss a detail, but I have, a rather large one, and it could mean the end of the road for both of us.

I have to use power, I have no choice. But when I try to smother his wolf, it pushes back against me.

STARVING. He tries to rise. I can't stop him so I go with him, but when we reach the aisle, I turn him with force, pushing him toward the back of the plane. He fights me, head down, snarling. We win a few startled looks from passengers as we go by, but fortunately, most of them are wearing headsets, watching movies, distracted from the real and dangerous show walking past them.

The bathroom stall on the right is full, but the one on the left is empty. I catch a shocked glance from a flight attendant as I push Sage into the stall and go in after him, locking the door behind me. There's barely enough room for us both, worse with Sage's wolf trying desperately to emerge. I pin him to the toilet seat and sit in his lap, straddling him, holding him down physically and with magic. The wolf fights me, argues, snarls.

No. I pin him with power, forcing the wolf to stop. His hands are claws now, fur growing on his cheeks. His eyes are full of power, canine and angry. I continue to smother him as best I can, soothing him instead of rousing my own rage. He responds at last, panting out his elongated mouth, not quite a snout, and it begins to retreat.

"Open the door, please!" The flight attendant pounds on the flimsy barrier between us and her.

"He's very sick." I feel his anger resurface. Damn her and her terrible timing.

"Please, open the door." She sounds mad herself.

Sage. I whisper in his mind. *You have to take control. Or we're in huge trouble.*

He growls in my mind, but I can feel him doing his best while the attendant continues to bang on the door. Another joins her, two voices whispering and then a male voice joins hers.

"You must open the door immediately," the man

says.

Sage gulps a breath and pushes. The wolf retreats in a rush, snapping at me, but finally giving in. Something clicks and the lock turns from the outside. I turn to find the two attendants staring at us. The woman looks nervous and angry, but her male counterpart just looks embarrassed.

"Sorry," I say, climbing off Sage. I know what this looks like, and the best thing to do is play along. "We're done now."

The woman tsks while the man sighs and steps aside. "If we were still over land, you'd be removed from the plane. As it is, consider yourselves warned."

I shrug casually, smiling up at him with my best sultry eyes. "Yes, sir," I say. I take Sage's hand and lead him back to our seats. He sinks into his by the window, face pale, but body hot. The act is no longer necessary. I drop it and lean in. "Are you okay?"

Sage nods, swallows hard. "I'm losing me," he whispers.

"You'll be fine," I say. "It was the smell of food. If you eat, you'll be okay."

Sage doesn't look hopeful and I wish I wasn't lying to him. Getting him something to eat will help, yes. But his wolf will only become stronger and stronger until I lose him completely.

If he's a revenant. And if he's some new kind, what

then? What happens to Sage? If he turns out like Caine, I'll kill him myself.

I lean out into the aisle to attract the flight attendant's attention. At least I can stave this off and go one step at a time. She looks irritated, but heads my way. I turn back, reaching for the menu card, to ask Sage what he'd like—more meat, the better—when I catch a face looking back at me from first class.

My stomach clenches, hands knotting around the menu the instant Jean Marc Dumont's smiling face registers.

TWELVE

Sage feels my concern just as the attendant reaches me.

"Can I help you?" She's trying to be polite, but it's obvious she'd rather kick me off the plane. I look up at her, still in shock, and hold out the card.

"He's starving," I say, my American accent slipping a moment. "Whatever you have with meat in it."

She frowns, about to argue.

"I know we're supposed to wait for the cart," I say. "But please. If you could?"

She sighs heavily, but nods and walks away. Sage leans in to me, scowling as I lower my head and breathe slowly through my mouth to calm myself.

"What?" His tension mirrors mine.

"We're not alone." I know if I look back up the

aisle, through the partially open curtain, I'll see Jean Marc again. And likely Kristophe. And those two don't travel alone. Which means…

Andre is on the plane with me.

I'm trapped.

—in a cage, crouched in filth, my body aching from beatings and other things, my mouth dry and hot with illness I'm just recovering from. I don't know how much more I can take, but my wolf demands we survive, so I let her take over. Let her be the one who paces the inside of the tiny enclosure, shoulders hunched forward, long, blonde hair hanging in scraggly strings to brush the dirty straw on the stone floor. Waiting for him to come back—

Someone stirs up front, breaking the memory in half, allowing me to return to myself. I raise my eyes in total dread, my wolf knowing, me, the girl inside me, all of us well aware of what's coming, of who is coming. My heart beats rapidly, a tiny bird in panic, the whole world narrowing to a tunnel of black, the center of it inhabited by the tall, angular form of the man I've known most of my life.

—he's come back, back to hurt me some more. Back to add to my torment, to teach me, offer me an education, he calls it. But my soul only hardens against him with every visit. And I grow stronger for the abuse—

Strong, yes. But terrified none the less. Of Andre Dumont.

He stands from his first class seat, adjusting his suit

coat as though such things matter, decorum and appearances. It gives me a moment to draw air into my lungs through my gaping mouth, gone dry from memory, hands clenching in my lap. He lazily turns and walks down the aisle, through the curtain, Jean Marc and Kristophe grinning at me around the backs of their seats. I ignore them, doing everything I can to hold myself together, as Andre's shiny shoes stop next to me. The scent of him washes over me, choking the little air I'm able to draw.

—*he smells of sandalwood and vanilla. I will never be able to bear that smell again—*

And to the empty seat beside me.

He settles into it, crossing his legs, a soft smile on his face, as fake as the rest of him. I can see the fine lines showing in his carefully maintained illusion of youth. He hasn't gone so far as his insane mother, Odette, who used massive doses of family power to disguise her decline. But he's not going easily into age, his skin thinning on his cheeks, the lids falling ever so slightly over his icy eyes. Age will not treat Andre well, I can only imagine. And hope.

I still can't believe there was an instant when I was a child I thought him handsome. With his aristocratic features and ice blond hair, his intense blue eyes and polished demeanor, I wondered when I was given to him if he would be a good master, someone honorable I could bond to without regret, with pride in my pairing.

I was so wrong.

Andre doesn't try to touch me, simply smiles, looking back and forth between Sage and me. The attendant arrives with a sub sandwich wrapped in foil. I pay for it with trembling fingers, hating the traitor way my hand shakes in front of the man I hate the most in this world, the monster who made me what I am. It burns in my soul Andre sees my upset. The attendant leaves us alone as Sage devours the sandwich in giant bites. I know he can't control himself, but I despise the way Andre watches him with cold calculation, a tiny smirk lifting the corner of his mouth while his empty blue eyes measure Sage's state of being.

"So lovely to finally find a moment alone with you." Andre's French accent always gives me the creeps, reminds me of being a little girl again, unable to fight back. And though I know it's not their fault, every time I hear a French accent now, I have a hateful reaction to whomever is speaking.

"What do you want?" It's obvious he's managed to trap me here. But there are no Enforcers I can feel, no pressure of threatening magic. Even Andre's is dormant, without challenge against my shields. Which means the Dumont leader has plans of his own that don't involve the authorities.

"I've done my best to keep them from finding you,"

he says, the most shocking thing I've heard leave his mouth in a long time. "Seems to have worked, when you've not chosen to be a stupid girl and get others involved."

I'm still a girl to him. And though I wish she would stop her savage screeching inside me, I have no control over the screams of the very child he speaks of.

"You've been protecting us?" Not very damned likely. Unless… "Why?"

"I would think that would be obvious, my dear Charlotte." His smile turns sharp and cruel. "You are in a position that puts me at an advantage. No one else can save you and get away with it, not even your beloved Sydlynn. They would guess where you've gone, watching her closely, the Enforcers." He nods as I silently curse. "Yes, even on my new adopted continent. Erica Plower and the North American Council are on watch for you as well. Though they have no idea how close you've come to leaving Europe. At least, not yet."

I glare at him, wishing I could stop the trembling that has taken over my body.

"Now," he says, brusque, but cheerful, "*mon animal de compagnie*," he loved calling me his little pet, "to answer your question. Since you can't go home, and have nowhere to turn, you are out of options. I'm going to give you one." He straightens his tie, plays with his cuff links, hooded eyes making my stomach churn. "I help you," he says, "because I want you for myself."

The girl in me wails her denial, terror breaking out sweat all over my body. It is only sheer force of will keeping me from attacking him.

"I know you better than those fool Enforcers," Andre says. "I've been following your lovely scent ever since you left the palace. No one knows you like I do. And no one deserves to own you, but me."

Never again. Never. Never. Never. Never—

"I want you to come work for me." I know what that means. "Work" equals "slave" to Andre. "And, in return, I'll protect your *petite* pet project," he flicks his fingers at Sage who glares with wolf eyes, still chewing his sandwich. "I'll even do my best to find a way to save him, if that pleases you."

Why would he do that? "I don't believe you." He's never given me a reason to trust him. The opposite, in fact. I fight memories, the girl inside me wanting to fall into the darkness of them, but I can't do it. I have to stay present, if only for Sage.

"Believe me or not," Andre says, "it's the truth." He leans toward me despite Sage's rumbled growl of a warning. "I owned you once," he hisses in my ear. "And I will own you again, Charlotte Girard. Mark me."

—I crouch, naked, in a corner, my tiny girl's body shifting into wereform as Andre laughs, shedding his belt, pulling at the zipper of his expensive dress pants—

I jerk back from him, though his hand grasps my wrist and holds me.

"That's the deal," he says. "I save your revenant, keep him safe, and you submit to me."

I can't, I can't, but how can I not? I turn to look at Sage who shakes his head, wolf eyes retreating.

"It's not worth it," he says.

"You don't have a choice." Andre releases me. "I have you trapped on board this plane. One message from me, and the Enforcers will come. Say no, and your boyfriend dies in fire. Say yes, and I keep them from him."

"Or I kill you and your filthy children." I've never felt so fierce. Is it Sage's influence? But now the girl in me is no longer afraid. She's furious.

Andre flinches a little, just enough I know I've scared him. "You can try," he says. "And the boy dies. You can't take all of us out at once without making a scene in front of normals. And if anything happens to me or *mes fils*, the revenant will suffer for it."

No, I won't be trapped. But I am, and I allowed it to happen.

Despair surges inside me, the old hurts waking and trying to swallow me. The little girl I was wails her desperation. I turn to Sage, feeling panic devouring me. I reach for his hand, feel his fear for me, not for himself.

Charlotte, his mind touches mine.

I can't let him die.

But I can't give in to Andre.

Cold fingers run over my cheek. I turn my head, meet those ice blue eyes and something in me snaps.

My power surges, reaching for rescue. And finds the veil between planes. I jerk at it, a desperate action, and I'm suddenly falling through a slice in the veil, seatbelt doing nothing to hold me in place, Sage held tightly to my hand.

My last view before darkness is Andre's angry face disappearing as the tear snaps closed.

THIRTEEN

I'm falling in the dark, but it's far different than the sorcery tunnel I'm used to. The veil has never felt this way before, so empty and loose, the rubbery membrane not holding me in place, but flowing around me like a thick river. I know I have some kind of demon connection, thanks to the trip I took to Demonicon with Syd. She claims I have access to that power, through fire, and I felt it, have used it in the past to speed my steps when in werewolf form. And I've even experienced the zing of it when I ride the veil with Syd. But, there's a purpose to our movement when I travel with my friend, a firm grasp of magic keeping us on target. This simply has the sensation of being lost in the vastness of nothing, sucked down deeper and deeper with no end in sight, the burn of the demon power inside me nowhere to be felt.

My panic still holds, as tightly as I cling to Sage's hand. I barely see him, even with my wolf senses at maximum. It's impossible to stop my mind from screaming its distress into the emptiness of the veil between planes.

I don't know what happens to those who enter the veil but don't come out the other end. But I can make an educated guess. The veil is vast, connecting thousands of planes. Sage and I could fall forever and never escape. My mind flashes to Syd, the night she was drained by Batsheva Moromond and her vampires, having enough power to enter the veil but not enough to leave it.

I was certain we lost her, that Syd was gone forever, devoured by the veil. And I think had she not connected with Max, with Trill Zornov, she would have perished no matter her near imperviousness to harm.

Sage and I have no such protections.

We're going to die here.

PLEASE! I send the word out in a burst of desperate hope. *Save us!* All of my pride is gone, my need to protect my hardened core from showing weakness. I can't let our lives end here in the darkness. This would be a terrible end.

Silence and falling and the suctioning nothingness of the veil. Not even Syd can hear me here. I give up hope, though my mind continues to beg the Universe for help. It's all I can do. I turn to Sage, see his lips moving, but I can't hear his words, the sound swallowed by the veil. I pull him closer, hug him tightly to me.

It can't end this way.

Something buffets against me, wind moving where there is no wind.

I beg you, a soft mind says as a gray figure with giant wings and glowing diamond eyes comes to hover in front of me, huge dragon nose practically touching mine. *Stop with the noise you're making, if you don't mind.*

My mental shriek cuts off, panic retreating. *Max?*

I am not my leader, the drach says, the pressure of his wing strokes halting our downward tumble. I hear Sage's mental churning in my head now I've stopped screaming, the veil making it easier to connect with him when I'm focused. He's trying to grasp the vision of a dragon hovering before us, but I don't have time to comfort him.

We are lost, I send to the drach, almost sobbing my relief. *Can you help?* Sanity returns with the fading memory of Andre, with the fear of our endless deaths now gone. We've escaped, somehow, I recall. Through a tear in the veil. Did I do that? I did that…

Odd, the drach says in a conversational tone, as though we weren't hovering in the veil, but standing on an ordinary street corner passing the time of day. *One would think if you can enter the veil, you could exit it on your own power as well.*

It was an accident. How did I do it? I must find out,

desperation shoved aside by a blast of victory. This could solve many problems for Sage and me. Panic is replaced by hope for our future.

I see. The drach sweeps his wings again, rainbow light casting off him and sparking in the veil. *You are a werewolf?*

I am, I send. *A dear friend of Sydlynn Hayle.* I'm not above using that relationship in this moment, though I second-guess myself once I say her name. Hopefully, he won't summon her or worse, Max. I'm certain the leader of the drach will insist on taking me to Wilding Springs.

Indeed, the drach says. *Any friend of the Light One is a friend of the drach. You had a destination in mind when this accident occurred?*

I reach out and brush my fingers over the rock-hard scales of his nose. *Yes*, I send, my mind going to Miami. I realize my mistake the moment the veil opens beside us and the shining night-time coast of Florida appears. But I have no time to ask the drach to take us further.

Be well, friend of Sydlynn Hayle, he sends.

And we're plunging ten feet toward the ground, landing hard on damp sand as the heavy waves pound froth upon the shore behind us. Sage pants into the warm night air, looking up as I do in time to see the veil seal itself again.

"Damn it!" I pound the ground with both fists. "I'm an idiot!"

Sage rolls over onto his back, coughing a laugh. "You saved our lives," he says. "What's so wrong with that?"

"I should have told him to send us to California." I sit up, brushing sand from my arms, shaking my dark bob in frustration. "What a waste of an opportunity."

Sage props himself up on one elbow, grinning. "The coolest freaking save in the history of saves," he says, "and you're still not happy."

I meet his eyes, catch my lips lifting with my mood. "Well," I say, "it was rather awesome." I can tear the veil. Me, Charlotte. I can do what Syd does, what I know Andre can't do. That brings me great satisfaction. He needs magic to travel, visible magic. I can use the veil.

Now I just need to figure out how to do it under controlled circumstances. And how to make an exit point on the other side. Because I can't be guaranteed there will be another drach around next time to save us.

"Come on," I say, climbing to my feet, helping Sage to his. "We've got a fair head start on Andre, but he may have altered the North American Enforcers by now."

Sage frowns at me, eyes shifting slightly and back again. "I get the impression he won't turn us in."

A shiver runs down my back, makes my toes curl. I can't let the man affect me anymore. I'm no longer that girl he tortured and abused. If only I can convince her of that. "No matter," I say. "We've covered a lot of ground.

But we still have a country to traverse."

Sage doesn't comment as I turn to scan the well-lit Miami skyline. I haven't been here in years, since I almost died, returning to find my bond to Syd was broken and gone with my near-death experience. Andre had been there that night, the night Syd destroyed the machine the Brotherhood used to steal the Dumont power. He deposed Mia, took control of the family magic himself. And now, he's the first male coven leader in the history of coven leaders.

Syd told me later she almost took the power for herself, as risky as that would have been. I wish she had and killed Andre in the process. But no, I want that particular thrill for myself. I don't know when or how, but I will see to it Andre Dumont doesn't see the old age he's obviously worried about.

I shudder again despite my determination as we make our way up the beach and to the boardwalk. Whatever Andre's reasons for wanting control of me, it will never happen. I'll put an end to my life—and Sage's—before I allow the Dumont leader to take me.

FOURTEEN

The street bustles with tourist activity, six hours or so behind where we just left. The night is still young, fresh. But I haven't forgotten Sage's internal clock. It has no use for time zones. We may have gained a few hours, but he's still on day four with time running short.

"Now what?" Sage looks up and down the street, turning sideways to block me from a group of teenagers. "We've lost all our stuff."

Our carryons are gone, left behind on the airplane. No money, no papers. But we don't need passports anymore, at least. Money, on the other hand...

"You," I say to him, pushing him toward a small café, open to the air, an empty table next to the sidewalk. I still have the change in the pocket of my dress from paying for his sandwich. "Have a coffee. I'll be right back."

Sage's frown tells me he knows what I'm up to, but he doesn't argue. I leave him as a girl comes to wait on him, watch a moment as he smiles at her, makes her blush. He's so good with people, so genuine everyone adores him.

I have to save him.

Though I'm not proud of these particular skills, I've been well trained as a pickpocket. In fact, it was the first thing I learned as a young girl, taught by one of the Black Souls. He thought it amusing to teach the young of the werenation to steal, the mighty werewolves reduced to taking pocket change from strangers. And though I'm a bit out of practice, I was always the best of my age group. With a few brushes by tourists and accidental bumps into the odd rich girl with her tiny clutch dangling from her hip, I have more than enough wallets to mine for what I need.

I take a moment in a dark alley behind an oriental restaurant to sift through my gains. The wallets and all their plastic go in the dumpster beside me, while the cash makes a comforting wad in the padding of my bra. Two thousand or so, rich girl's coin purse the most generous, more than enough to carry us across the country without a problem.

Sage doesn't comment when I stroll up to him, just stands and follows me, leaving a generous tip beside his barely touched cup of coffee. It's not until we round the corner he takes my hand and sighs.

"All set?" At least he's not arguing with me this time.

"One more thing to do and we're ready to go." I spot exactly what I'm looking for in a large parking lot across the street. We saunter over to the small econobox like we own it. Sage's scowl never leaves him while my hands search the door handle. A touch of power and it's unlocked, power I mask as carefully as I can. They might know we're off the plane, but the Enforcers will have no idea where we ended up. As long as I'm not the only werewolf on the continent—I know for certain I'm not— this small dose of magic shouldn't be noticed.

I hope.

The engine fires easily, and I grin at the full tank of gas. Whoever the owner is, I send them a thank you into the night as I pull out and onto the street, heading north and west.

"Next stop, California," I say, trying to be cheerful.

Sage nods, looking out the passenger window. I focus on driving through the busy Miami streets, on the pedestrians and flashing lights that distract me. So, when Sage turns to me, I'm surprised by his anger.

"When this is over," he says, "I don't ever want to steal anything ever again."

It's hard not to glare back at him. He's lucky, in fact,

I'm busy with driving or he'd get a healthy smack for being an ass. "I already told you," I say. "I'll do anything to save you."

"Fine," he says, crossing his arms over his chest, "and I'm okay with that. But promise me."

"You think I'm enjoying this?" Maybe a little, but he doesn't have to know that. I take pride in how well I've been trained, how well I do my job. But he's more than a job to me, and I love him too much to let this get between us.

"I don't know." Sage sighs, lets his arms go. "I just want this to be over." He winces, rolls his left shoulder.

"Me, too," I say. We come to a stop light and I bite my lower lip, wondering. "There could be another way." Can I figure it out? How to transport us through the veil? Maybe, if we find a quiet place I can try it.

"That hole you made in the air?" He turns to me.

"It's called the veil," I say as we start moving again. The lights are bright in my eyes as I talk, cars flashing by. "It is the place between planes."

"Planes." Sage sounds confused, and I hardly blame him.

"There's a lot more I haven't told you," I say.

He sits back with that sexy grin of his. "We have a long drive and lots of time."

Maybe not, if I can figure this out. When we come to the next light, I pull over into a gas station parking lot.

I turn to him when I park, taking his hand in mine.

"Okay," I say, "here it is. There are thousands of worlds, all connected by the veil. It's like a curtain keeping all the planes apart. But there are certain people who can cut through it and even use it to travel from place to place. Or plane to plane."

Sage swallows, nods. "Got it," he says. "Not sure I believe it, but okay."

I roll my eyes. "You've been in it, met a drach, and you still don't believe?"

He swallows again. "Right, the dragon. I forgot about him."

I laugh, I can't help myself. "He's called a drach," I say. "And you're taking this very well."

Sage answers my laugh with a shaky one of his own, green eyes almost glowing in a trick of the light coming from the gas station through the car window. "Do I have any choice?"

"I've never been able to use the veil before," I say. "Syd's an old pro at it, and Piers. But he uses a different method than we do." I don't have time to explain all the different kinds of magic to him, not now. "My fear must have given me the boost I needed to cut through."

"But without an exit," Sage says.

I nod. "Because I didn't have a plan," I say. "I just wanted to get away from Andre. And save you."

Sage's eyes narrow, hand tightening around mine.

"You're going to have to tell me what he did to you."

Not a chance. "If I can figure out how I did it," I say, "access it consciously, we can dump this car right now and go direct to California."

"No dragons?" Sage winks, grins, but he's shaking a little. So brave, my love.

"Hopefully not this time," I say. I reach inside as he watches me. I can feel his focus on me, his tension through the connection of our hands.

"What, now?" His voice squeaks slightly as the pitch rises.

"No time like it," I say. "Now shush."

It's there, I feel it as I focus. The veil is right there next to me, all around me, and my magic is tied to it now. As though traveling through it once made the difference. This could work. To get to California now, tonight, with three days to spare... I'm sure I can find the answers I need in time.

But no matter how hard I pull, push, tug, cut, the veil remains closed to me. Frustration builds into an almost tangible thing inside the cabin of the little car until I finally open my eyes and blink into the bright lights of the gas station's exterior.

"Slow way, huh?" Sage pulls me to him, kisses my forehead. "It's okay, Charlie."

I shake my head, fury replacing frustration a moment, wolf flaring in my eyes. I slam both hands down on the steering wheel before staring the engine.

Useless. We have a long drive ahead of us and I've just lost us two days in travel because I can't figure out how to use my power properly.

It's a quiet drive into the south Florida night.

FIFTEEN

The blush of dawn greets me in the rear-view as I push the pedal down and make the best time I can on the Florida interstate. We're almost to Louisiana, but my hands want to steer north. It's only a half day's drive to Pennsylvania, to Wilding Springs. But it's almost thirty more hours to Los Angeles. I'm insane, thinking I can do this on my own. I don't even have to drive, I can just open my shields and call for Syd. She'll be here in moments.

But I can't. She has her own Council to listen to, her own laws to follow, despite her insistence on autonomy. I won't risk her family, or mine, not until I have the proof I need of Caine and his pack's revenant status and, hopefully, a cure for Sage.

He stirs beside me, sleeping through part of the

drive, though restlessly. I've stopped him from clawing at his shoulder twice now, in his sleep, but he remained out cold so I let him stay that way. I'm tired, but I've endured worse. As soon as I find a place to pull over for food and a rest stop, I will. Maybe catch a few hours of sleep. But first, I need to replace the license plates on this car so we don't get pulled over. Bad enough we're hunted by Enforcers. It would just add insult to injury having to deal with normal law enforcement because I overlooked something as simple as stolen plates.

Ten minutes later, just on the other side of the Louisiana border, I pull over into a small gas station. Sage stirs as I park at the pump, eyes a wolf's eyes in the moment of his waking. But he smiles and the wolf fades, the musky scent wafting out of the car as I open the door.

I leave him to pump gas, slipping around the back side of the station. It's one of those combo service and gas stations with a few old cars in the weeds behind the building. A quick theft of some Louisiana plates from a clunky old truck and my job is done.

A plastic bag of junk food lands in Sage's lap when I climb in. The cute girl behind the counter grinned at me when I loaded the packaged sandwiches, assorted snacks and big bags of chips on the counter, her sparkly made-up gaze going out the window to Sage.

I winked at her before returning to the car.

He tears into the first sleeve of chicken salad,

helping himself in alternate bites to a full chunk of beef jerky while I drive off. Half a mile later, I pull over to switch out the plates and we're on our way again.

But as I head back to the driver's seat, I find Sage already claimed it.

"You're bagged," he says. "And I'm fine." He sounds it, and when I let my power touch him, realize he feels it, too. Almost chipper, his energy high, the scent of him almost happy. "I drive, you snooze." I hesitate one last moment, whipping the bad plates into the woods on the side of the road. "Charlotte," he says, voice dropping, "I mean it. I'm counting on you, remember?" Guilt. He uses guilt at a time like this. "Now, get in that seat and get some sleep before you fall over."

I pause still. There's no telling when a new round of change could take over. But he's well fed and rested and showing no signs of pain anymore. Could he be recovering? Impossible, but I do need sleep.

"Wake me the moment something happens." I fasten my seatbelt and recline, worried I'm making a terrible mistake.

"You mean if," Sage says, pulling out onto the country road, heading for the interstate.

"I hope it's 'if,'" I say, closing my eyes, "but I know better." And yet, luck has been on our side, has it not?

Regardless of my worry, sleep comes quickly and easily.

I open my eyes, wide awake, as the car comes to a halt. I sit up, find the sun is setting in front of us. A small building surrounded by a parking lot and picnic tables squats before us, several large trucks pulling in and out.

A rest stop. I turn to Sage who unbuckles his belt. He smiles at me, but his face looks pale, cheeks bright at the bones with pink spots. I reach for him, but he dodges me.

"Right back," he says. He leaves me in the car, heading for the building and the washroom. I follow slowly, stretching out my muscles. He's driven all day. I should have told him to wake me long before now. It's clear he's in pain again, from the washed-out look on his face.

No more. I'm driving from here on in. The sleep I've gained has given me the momentum I need to see us through to California.

I return to the car to find Sage in the back seat, eating again. He looks up as I climb in next to him. He's parked us away from the lights surrounding the building, in a tiny pocket of darkness. I take the opportunity to snuggle up against him, happy to find a blanket on the floor at my feet. I pick at a sandwich while he finishes the rest of the food, my stomach happier for the sustenance.

Done, I toss the container aside and sigh, sinking back against the seat. We need to go, but it's comfortable here with him, quiet and dark and peaceful. Sage pulls me against him, shares the last of the food with me. Sweet chocolate does the rest of the job reviving me, as much as the water I splashed on my face, the damp paper towels I used to wipe down. It's not a shower and fresh clothes, but it will do.

"Charlotte." I turn to look up at Sage. He's staring down at me with a little smile, though he still seems pale to me. "In all of this, I've forgotten to thank you for saving my life."

"And don't you forget it." I poke him softly in the stomach, brushing chip crumbs from his shirt. "You're welcome. But we're not out of this yet."

Sage nods, pulling me closer. "Do you really think I can be healed?"

I don't know how to answer.

"If you do," he says, "I want to stay a werewolf." His lips descending over mine. "So I can be with you forever. I love you, Charlotte." He doesn't give me the chance to answer, sadness crawling out of the pit in my gut. "But just in case it goes the other way," he whispers over my mouth. "I want you to know how grateful I am."

We don't have time for this, but I can't bring myself to reject him, not when my body and heart and soul crave him with every touch of his skin against mine. It's insane and foolish. We're on the run, in a rest stop on an interstate with the world going on around us. But when

Sage kisses me again, I slip into his lap, straddling him, pulling the blanket over both of us.

It's not romantic or private. But it's all we've got. And I won't squander this chance to be with Sage.

SIXTEEN

I drive into the night, Sage quiet beside me, the miles passing under the wheels of our stolen car. I stopped in Texas to change out the plates again, just in case, but there's been no sign of pursuit, neither the normal kind nor the touch of Enforcers. So Andre has chosen to keep his mouth shut.

I just wished knowing that made me feel better.

Sage has been quiet since we left the rest stop, since our rapid love-making left us both panting and wanting more. I long to pull over into one of the small motels off the interstate and spend one last night with him. How lovely it could be, with his wolf emerging. I wouldn't have to hold back. That thought startles me. I've always been so careful with him, for fear of doing something, out of passion, we'd both regret. My wolf understood, always, and still does. Now I realize such restraint is unnecessary.

Still, what would unbridled passion do to him? Would it speed up the process? His wolf emerged when he climaxed in the back seat, but only for a moment. If I were to let mine out, allow her to connect with him…

Too risky. And yet incredibly tempting. Which leads me to other thoughts I can't have. Thoughts of being a queen, but this time with smiling Sage at my side, our beautiful children raised to pride and honor, but to love themselves and be free, first and foremost.

It's a lovely dream. I only wish there was a chance in hell it could ever come true.

As for pulling over, I know it's a foolish idea. I just can't spare the time. We have to reach California as fast as we can. Because no matter Sage's questions, his request to remain a werewolf if he's healed, he is and will always be a revenant, a werewolf who has been made and not born. And though we might be able to convince the powers that be to keep him alive if a cure is found, there is no way I'll be able to take him as my mate.

The dream dies, but I won't wallow in the older version, where I'm a slave to the throne. I won't. It may come, but not here. I won't think about my future now. There's too much road ahead of us, figurative and literal, for me to stray from my focus. Find a way to help him first. Then figure the rest out later. First things first.

Sage stirs beside me as the sign for San Antonio

flashes in my headlights. He grins at me, lop sided, but for the first time I notice how red his face is. I've missed it in my distraction, so many details I've let slip. His paleness has gone, replaced by fever, his skin tight and shining red. And the scent of him has changed. I was so wrapped up in my thoughts I missed the shift completely.

He suddenly smells ill.

I reach out, touch his face, wince at how hot he feels. He's burning up, the wolf in him super heating his insides as it battles the infection—which means, it's either fighting itself, or he's contracted some other bacteria or virus that's interfering. When I glance at his shoulder, I see his T-shirt is soaked, the infection seeping through.

"Sage," I say, accusation in my voice, though it's not his fault. "Why didn't you say something?"

He shakes his head, wobbly, smile child-like. "Charlie." He slurs my name. "Hiya, Charlie."

I take the next exit too fast, the tires squealing under the car, but I'm not thinking about my driving. I have to get him medicine, find a way to reduce his fever. Were he a full werewolf, I wouldn't worry. His lupine nature would take care of things. Then again, were he a werewolf, he wouldn't be this sick in the first place.

His wolf is rising, but it's not enough. Yes, the sickness might yet burn off. The wolf is strong in him and, though he's sick, I can't sense the taint I've associated with revenants in the past. But it's possible the infection he's fighting—both of them—could trigger something else entirely. I have so little knowledge of what is actually happening to him, I can't make a judgment either way. But the realization a trauma like this could trigger a shift in him decides for me.

I can't allow the revenant to win before I can find a cure.

We're in downtown San Antonio, surrounded by cars, stopped at a streetlight. I barely remember driving this far. I have to focus. My gaze sweeps both sides of the street, rewarded at last. I spot a little pharmacy on a corner and park across the street, ignoring the angry beeping of the cars trying to get around me. I should leave him here, but I can't risk it. What if he were to change right here in traffic? I'd never get to him in time, before someone took a photo or video. And with today's social media sites, he'd be all over the world before even the witch councils could stop it.

I spin on him, unbuckling his belt, leaning over to open his door. A firm shove gets him moving, wobbly but functional. I climb out after him, partly to avoid the traffic swerving around the car, and partly to keep him from falling down. Sage sways on the sidewalk, leaning to the left, still with that goofy grin on his face.

The traffic thins a moment, a woman giving me the finger before gunning past. I take advantage of the gap, dragging Sage across the street and to the glass door of the pharmacy. He wavers next to me, head down, barely registering the chime of the bell overhead as we enter with a soft whimper.

I keep him close to me as I hurry down the aisles, hands grabbing for pain killers. But what I really need are antibiotics, and I don't have access. What will they do to his wolf physiology? I have no idea. But his human side needs them, that much is obvious. My gaze whips to the back of the store and the prescription counter. An older man stands there in a crisp white coat, balding head gray in a ring around his temples. He hasn't noticed us, absorbed in whatever he's working on, a pen in his hand. I know he won't give me what I need, not without a prescription. He's not allowed, it's human law.

Which means I might have to hurt him to help Sage.

As I turn to tell my love to stay put, he pulls away from me, lunging forward, strength renewed as the fever rages. His eyes have gone wolf, hands grasping at random items. He sniffs them with aggressive interest, casting things aside almost as quickly as he seizes them. I can't risk controlling him with magic, and am forced to chase him as he leaps forward and into the path of a young woman. She screams at the sight of him, her high heels slipping on the tile, short skirt hitching upward as she totters. I grab for her, pull her upright by her bare arm. She runs with clacking feet, hands scrambling over the keypad of her phone.

I look up and realize we're no longer anonymous. We've caught the frowning attention of the pharmacist whose hand hovers over a phone of his own.

Damn it, I have to control Sage before this devolves further. But he lunges out of my reach as I dive for him, skidding into the empty space in front of the pharmacy counter. He grins, panting, at the older man, licking his lips as though the pharmacist is dinner. And then, Sage spins in place, eyes rolling up into his head, before collapsing to the floor like a broken rag doll.

His heart skips. Stops. Stutters. Stops again.

No, please no. He can't be dead—

I'm frozen in place, even as the world erupts around me. A slim black woman with finely braided hair tied at the nape of her neck falls to her knees next to Sage before looking up at the pharmacist.

"Call an ambulance," she snaps with authority.

This can't be happening. I rush forward, try to pull her off Sage as his heartbeat returns, but she shoves me back, dark eyes snapping with anger. "Are you with him?"

I can only nod, mute and shaking.

"He needs to go to the hospital." She talks to me as though I'm a child, or unable to understand simple concepts. And, at the moment, I'm both. He can't go to a normal hospital. They will run tests, on his blood, his makeup—

I have to get him out of here.

But a siren is already loudly approaching, an ambulance pulling up to the door, people whispering and staring as a pair of paramedics with a stretcher run into the store, and the young black woman is directing them what to tell the emergency room. Her words are garbled, unintelligible as time slows and flexes and speeds again. I reach for her as they start to wheel Sage away.

"Go with him," she says. "I'll meet you there."

"Why?" I'm shaking all over. This can't be happening, not now.

"I'm Dr. Lauren Mitchell," she says. "Just trust me."

She pushes me toward the door and I run on autopilot, gaze settling on our stolen car across the street one last time before I climb stiffly into the back of the ambulance, eyes locking on Sage's silent face.

SEVENTEEN

I pace the waiting room, body vibrating with nerves as the bustling hospital sounds and scents add to the overload. The pungent smell of cleaners does little to mask the heavy weight of sickness hanging over the building, and though I push my wolf back as far as I can, my sensitive nose is assaulted over and over again, driving me mad.

It makes focus almost impossible, the air hard to breathe. I need to figure out a new plan, something I find increasingly frustrating as the weight of other people's illness settles on me like a solid presence. Our rapid drive to this place ended before I could work out how to liberate Sage from the hands of the paramedics. And the doctor from the pharmacy was already waiting for us when we arrived, her car screeching to a halt, her small body catapulting toward us as Sage was lowered to the ground. She practically leaped on Sage, escorting him into the hospital while I was held back, forced to deal with paperwork and questions about insurance and other things I barely understood let alone had answers to.

Insurance? Werewolves are never sick. And even if we did somehow contract an illness, magic is our first healing impulse, not this primitive use of foreign substances and crowding together the weak and weary behind four walls of growing pathogens. If the sickness that brings them here doesn't kill them, the insidious horrors mutating and lurking in the scent of cleansers not nearly strong enough for the job surely will.

I still have most of the two thousand dollars I'd stolen in Miami, enough to satisfy the busybody woman behind the desk. I have to use Syd's address when the receptionist asks, and hope doing so won't trigger some manhunt by accident. But no, Enforcers ignore normals, remember? Our biggest worry here is one of them finding out Sage isn't entirely human any longer.

I hate it here, but I can't leave him. And every time I try to seek him out beyond the cramped, crowded waiting area with its industrial tile floors and flickering florescent lights, I'm stopped at the double doors leading to emergency by a stern-faced nurse.

"The doctor will let you know when he can have visitors." I want to slap her aside with her bitter expression and her flat eyes, but she is just a product of this unnatural environment, trained to care only to a point.

When the slim black woman from the pharmacy finally appears, I rush to her, interrupting her whispered conversation with the same flat-eyed nurse. But her smile is at least genuine.

Dr. Mitchell pulls me aside, crisp, white lab coat hanging past her knees, the top of her head barely reaching my chin. She seems frail, delicate, but her aura is strong and, when we've reached a quiet corner, her personal power radiates from her face.

"We've had to put him on a heavy dose of antibiotics," she says. "He's also very dehydrated, so a saline drip and painkillers." She frowns for the first time, leaning closer, voice dropping to a whisper. "It's a serious infection. I've never seen anything like it. What the hell bit him?"

I can't tell her anything, and my churning mind won't manufacture a lie, so I don't say anything. Dr. Mitchell finally shrugs and leans back, a flicker of anger in her eyes.

"Fine," she says. "It's none of my business. And it's not a gun shot, so I don't have to report it. As long as no police requests for bite victim identification comes through while he's here, there's nothing I can do." Her gaze intensifies, as though waiting for me to confess some terrible crime. I continue to hold my tongue. She can't help us, not as a normal. But if her medicine can stabilize Sage, I'll allow him to remain.

For now.

"Listen to me." Her hand grips my elbow, fingers strong despite their slim, delicateness. "I have no idea what you two are into, but I figure it can't be good." She licks her lips before going on. "If you're running from something, and you've done nothing wrong, the police might be able to help." She shakes her head, braids rattling, the tiny beads on the ends clinking together. "I don't care about that," she says. "But I do care about my patient." Her hand tightens further. "If you try to take him out of here before the infection is gone, he'll die." She lets that sink in a moment. "Do you understand?"

I nod. There's nothing I can say. We need to go. Sage can't stay here. The last thing we need is for him to have a shift while in a normal hospital. That would bring Enforcers for certain, and cause a massive incident. But what if the doctor is right?

She lets me go. "You can see him now," she says. "He's sleeping. Please see to it he stays that way." Dr. Mitchell turns and walks away in quick, even strides, carrying the weight of the world on her shoulders with the authority of a queen. I hurry after her, through the doors into the treatment area.

The stench of sickness is stronger back here, but I

catch Sage's scent no matter the torment to my nose. He's a few beds down, screened off by a washed-out green curtain for a little privacy. I slip through, pulling the sheet tightly over the opening and go to his side.

He's pale, quiet, lips parched, eyes sunken. How did I not notice his decline? At least the fever seems to be gone. I grasp his cold, damp hand in mine and wrack my aching mind for a plan. My magic seeps out, just a tiny thread, to touch him. His heartbeat is strong, at least, no more stuttering. And the medicine seems to be pushing back the infection. But the wolf remains inside him, pacing and growling, wanting to emerge. No amount of antibiotics will keep it from its task.

Sage sighs, some color returning to his face as the wolf offers support. Werewolves are resilient, we can recover from almost any wound, given time. I wonder if this infection would have run its course without the medicine. Was I a fool to put us in this position? Would he have healed on his own? Too late to find out, now.

But one thing is certain. I have to get him out of here, no matter what Dr. Mitchell said. He's surfacing, and the wolf is coming with him.

Sage's eyes open, pupils huge, irises taking up most of the white, the wolf in him blinking slowly at me. But he smiles, squeezes my hand with strength, so I smile back and soothe his wolf with my own. It retreats, leaving my darling Sage behind.

"Charlie." His voice is hoarse, but his eyes are clear, untouched by fever or confusion. "Sorry about this."

I shake my head. "It's not your fault." I glance over my shoulder, to make sure we're still alone, though I know we are, before bending to kiss his cheek. And whisper in his ear. "We have to leave."

He nods, tries to rise, but I push him down again.

"Not yet." He's weak after all, his muscles shivering with the attempt to sit up. "Get some sleep first." I lean back. "A few hours, all right?"

Sage squirms, frowning. "We're running out of time."

"I know." I release his hand. "But if this medicine can keep you stable, we'll give it a chance to work."

He sinks into the pillow, eyes sad. "Are we going to make it?"

A nurse bustles in, brushing past me, fiddling with Sage's IV. She smiles at him, pats his arm. "You're looking better already."

"Thank you," he says with one of his dazzling smiles. The nurse turns to me with eyebrows raised.

"We just need a moment."

I nod, step back and out of the tent of curtains, letting her do her work. Pacing the hall will only get me kicked out, I'm sure. But the sight of a vending machine at the far end pulls me on. I'm suddenly thirsty and starving, the adrenaline of the last hour or so burning off.

I'm of no use to Sage if I'm collapsing, too.

A chicken sandwich and a cup of coffee later and I'm feeling more myself. Surely, the nurse is through with Sage by now. I return, observing the ward as I do. It's very busy back here, multiple doctors and nurses and orderlies in and out of the curtained areas. It won't be easy to sneak Sage out without someone seeing us. I'll have to find him some clothes, since they've taken his. Maybe some scrubs would disguise him well enough to get us past the staff.

I'm almost halfway back when I see someone enter Sage's section. He's in medical attire, but acts nervous, hand twitching on the curtain, pulling it shut behind him. And there's something about the set of his shoulders, the dirty blond hair, the way he walks that triggers memory.

I know him. And he's with Sage. A terrible combination.

I need to run, but I also need to keep a measured pace. No way am I alerting any of the normals something is amiss. My heart pounds so loudly I'm sure everyone in the hospital can hear it as I push my stride a little wider, covering more ground while keeping my posture casual. No time, I'm out of it, he's been in there with my love for seconds already. Anything could have happened. If the intruder is a werewolf, Sage could be dead. Or an Enforcer, Sage is probably gone.

But no, there's no flash of blue light, so it can't be

an Enforcer. Which means werewolf.

I feel the surge of nothing the moment I reach for the curtain and realize my mistake. Not a werewolf or a witch. That touch of empty means only one thing.

Sorcerer.

I'm inside the curtain, wolf emerging, holding it tightly closed behind me before the man hovering over Sage can turn around. A gaping black hole has opened next to the bed, widening as the sorcerer pours power into it. He looks up at me, scowling, and I finally make connections.

I've seen him before, several times. At Harvard, with Syd. In the basement of the Star Club, with Ameline. On the rooftop of Coterie Industries with Belaisle. In the morgue at Oxford, smiling at me through a closing door as I investigated revenant bodies. And now, here, trying to take Sage from me.

Rupe. Syd's old friend, who turned against her, joined the Brotherhood. And he's trying to steal my love.

EIGHTEEN

I lunge without thinking, across the end of the bed, both hands outstretched toward Rupe. He's not expecting a physical attack, clearly, because he flinches, raising both arms up to protect his face, letting go of Sage.

I hit him hard in the chest, knocking him back, but it's Sage who finishes the job. He turns sideways in bed, both feet lashing out, propelling Rupe off his feet and into the center of the black tunnel of power.

Rupe's shocked face vanishes as the way snaps shut behind him.

"Damn it." I turn to Sage who is now out of bed, shaking a little, but with a determined look on his face. "I should never have left you alone."

"Who was that?" He comes toward me, the gown he wears gaping in the back.

"The Brotherhood." I shiver. "They are involved." Syd needs to know. Rupe was one of Liander Belaisle's right hands, present at the last battle at the stronghold. He escaped with his master. Seeing him here confirms my fears.

"I have no idea who they are," Sage says, "but I take it this is bad."

I nod. "We have to go now."

I hate to leave him again, but I have no choice. A quick duck into a storage room turns up some scrubs I hope will fit and a hurried walk back to deliver them to Sage raises no eyebrows. I could use magic to make us less noticeable, but that will only encourage Enforcer interest. Why does everything have to be so hard?

Sage is much more stable when I hand over the scrubs, IV already pulled out, dressing quickly. I keep a careful eye out through the slit in the curtain while he does and almost jump when he touches my hand.

"Ready," he says.

Is he? I look into his eyes, touch his cheek. He feels all right, back in control. But how long will that last? The bandage over his shoulder isn't seeping anymore, so I'm going to have to trust we'll be okay.

We can't just walk out the front door. I wait until a nurse has passed and turn left, toward the vending machine. Sage follows me, head down. I'm tense, waiting for a shout to stop, security to come rushing at us. But no one seems to notice. We reach the end of the hall and the exit sign over a big, gray door.

The air outside is humid, but clear, and I can't help but draw a deep and cleansing breath. It's dark, but there are enough streetlights to make me nervous. A large parking lot lies across a flowerbed median and I head for it, planning to steal yet another car. This time, Sage doesn't look unhappy about it, glancing back over his shoulder as though Rupe could be there, ready to pounce.

We're barely across the first lane when the door slams behind us. I spin, primed to fight, Sage tense beside me, only to find Dr. Mitchell running toward us, fury on her face.

"What did I tell you?" She comes to a halt, vibrating with anger. She looks back and forth between Sage and I, suddenly startled, temper gone cold as she gapes at him. "That's impossible." She looks him over, reaches out and touches his arm, registers he's no longer boiling up. "How can you be standing, let alone healthy? You should still be out cold." She takes a half step back, though she's not afraid. Just lost, stunned, the medical world she knows shaken to its foundation. "Sage, you were dead. And now you're…" she shakes her head, looks at me with troubled eyes. "He was dead." She stresses the word. "I didn't tell you because he came back. I thought he was a goner. End of the line." She's babbling, one hand running over her damp forehead as her hands shake.

"And here you are." Dr. Mitchell's laugh is sharp, bordering hysterical. "Either you're a miracle, or there's a hell of a lot more going on here than you're telling me."

Instead of adding to her stress by trying to answer, Sage leans forward and shakes her trembling hand with one of his winning smiles lighting his eyes. "Thank you for taking such good care of me."

She nods, almost smiles, then seems to snap out of it. "Don't you wave those pearly whites at me." Her temper is back, she's in control again. I almost grin. She reminds me of me, needing to hold herself together in the face of the unknown. "What are you?"

Neither of us answer. We can't. Besides, she'd never believe us, or understand.

"Your blood tests came back." She's trembling all over again, but only for a moment. Her own adrenaline push is obviously wearing thin enough she'll suffer for it later.

More silence from us, while I wonder what they found in his blood.

Dr. Mitchell's face returns to anger, though she seems less enraged and more stern. "Never mind," she says. "It doesn't matter. I can't hold you here. Though I guess I could call security for stealing scrubs." I open my mouth to protest, hand reaching for what's left of the cash when she snorts, waves me off. Looks away, like she's making a decision she might regret later. Finally, she turns back to us, lips tight with disapproval. "I knew you'd pull something like this." She jerks a plastic bag from the pocket of her jacket and presses it into Sage's hand, dark eyes locked on his. "Every twelve hours, Sage. Do not miss a dose. And drink as much water as you can. You hear me?"

He steps forward and hugs her, surprising the doctor and me. "I promise."

She hugs him back, breathless when he releases her, touching her cheek where his lips brushed her skin. "Boy," she says, "I have no idea who or what you are, but for some reason, I have a feeling you'll be okay." Her dark gaze meets mine. "You take care of him," she says. "You take care of each other." Dr. Mitchell looks like she wants to say something else, thinks better of it. Before I can thank her, too, she turns and dashes for the door and doesn't look back.

Sage bounces the bag of medicine in his hand. He looks better than he has since he was bitten, and I feel relief things turned out the way they did.

"She's awesome." He grins at me, like this is some grand adventure and we just upped a level. I grin back, his good humor infectious, no pun intended.

I hook my arm through his and turn to the parking lot. "Time to find a new ride."

Sage bows to me. "Your highness," he says, gesturing with one hand, eyes twinkling. "Your chariot awaits."

We practically saunter across the second lane, spirits high. What has gotten into him? Into me? Whatever it is, I welcome it for as long as it lasts.

NINETEEN

The minivan I liberate is a newer model, the back seat filled with kid's toys. Sage finally hesitates at my choice, but I don't give him an option, or the chance to shatter our little bubble of happy I'm still clinging to. Instead, I point at the glove compartment.

"Find a name," I say, "and I'll make sure they not only get their van back, but they are compensated." That is, if I'm ever in a position to do so. It seems to make Sage feel better and he eagerly hunts for the registration.

San Antonio's glowing lights die behind us as we head onto the interstate again. I find myself constantly looking at Sage, checking him for signs of illness. He finally reaches out and squeezes my hand.

"I won't be stupid this time," he says. "The minute I feel weird, I'll tell you. And I'll take these." He slips the bottle of antibiotics from the plastic bag and holds it up. "And drink this." He shakes his Gatorade at me, a quick purchase from a corner store on our way out of the city. "You can stop worrying now."

"No," I say as we drive into the southern Texas night. "I'll never stop until you're cured."

He does feel stronger to me when I let my magic touch him, though I'm not sure that's a good thing. Because his wolf is stronger, too. At least he's still free of all traces of what I recognize as revenant. But what does that mean?

Day lights the sky behind us. I can't help but count down. This is the end of day five, eight hours behind my initial guess back home. Only two to go before the inevitable. I wish I hadn't lost the file Femke gave me. There is so much information I wish I had. But it's in my carryon, back in Miami, probably either in lost and found or confiscated by security by now.

Seven days, according to the file. But Sage is different, feels absolutely unique. So does that time frame still apply?

It's almost evening by the time I pull over into a gas station in the mountains. Texas came and went without incident, Arizona welcoming us. We're close to the California border, another eight or so hours to Los Angeles. If I drive all night, we'll be there by morning. Leaving me one day to find out who Caine and his people really are, though I now suspect who made them.

Belaisle and the Brotherhood. It has to be. I've tried a few times over the course of this day's drive to reach Syd and warn her, but without success. She's either shielding or not here on this plane. Which makes me even more nervous. I'm not going to ask her to rescue me, but knowing Syd is there in Wilding Springs is a huge comfort. If she's off somewhere with Max, which has often been the case the last few years, my safety net is gone. Selfish, really, but enough to trouble me. Besides, she really needs to know Belaisle is active again.

But why is he building werewolves? What does he want my people for? And why, if he's succeeded with Caine and his people, is he making such a mess of the revenants in Europe? It makes no sense.

The station is quiet, a few cars parked in front. Sage is sleeping, so I leave him to rest, climbing out to stretch and get gas. The tank full, I head inside to find us food and stock up on more water and juice for Sage.

The interior is rustic, and I immediately feel like an intruder as I enter. A small group of locals turns to stare as I walk toward the counter in the back. There's a small diner attached to the gas station, tables covered in plastic, wooden chairs and benches in desperate need of upholstery. But the food smells amazing and I find myself smiling as I greet the older woman behind the register.

She grins at me, thick hands jotting my order as I

salivate over the scent of cooking meat behind her. "That it, sweetie?" Her eyebrows go up as I add four hamburgers, two sausages and two large fries to the list of our dinner.

I hand her a wad of cash and grin. "My boyfriend is a beast," I say with a wink.

She laughs and winks back, ringing through my order. "Lucky girl."

I'm running low on cash, most of it gone to the hospital, though the moment we reach Los Angeles, I'll do some pick pocketing and rectify that. The gas bill takes up the last of it, leaving me with a handful of change rattling in the tip jar by the register.

It's colder here, and I'm still just in a little sundress, though the woman who owned the van was kind enough to leave a denim jacket in the back seat. It's big on me, but it's warmer than nothing. I ram my hands in my pockets as I wait for the food to cook, ignoring the stares of the locals, until they eventually turn away, bored by my inactivity.

The rumble of a big engine turns me around, a pick-up truck rolling past catching my attention. I miss the front as it passes, but the back is jacked up on giant tires, paint job old and dented.

Good old boys. How lovely.

Moments later, three big-bellied men with heavy beards, dressed in full camouflage enter the diner. The smell of wood smoke and blood drifts through the delightful scents of the space, making me immediately tense. I turn my back on them, staying close to the register, hoping they don't notice me. I know their type, all bravado and manliness. But maybe I'm wrong.

"Hey there, sweetheart." A heavy hand falls on my shoulder and I know I'm absolutely right after all. I turn to face the giant of a man, belly jutting toward me as he grins down through his dirty beard.

I shrug off his hand, looking away again. Damn it, I was hoping to keep this stop incident free. But if he touches me again, I'll hurt him.

His two buddies join him at the counter. The woman behind it scowls at them with a sympathetic look for me. "Mind yourself around my customers, Jake Wilkens, or I'll be calling the sheriff again."

Giant man grunts. "Don't have to be unfriendly," he says while his friends grumble agreement. "Was just saying hello, wasn't I?"

She shakes her pen at him. "I've had enough trouble with you and your boys," she says. "Now make an order and get your gas, or get your asses out of my place."

I grin at her, admiration for her skyrocketing. I can take care of myself, but it's nice to have a stranger look out for me for once. Happens rarely enough.

Before the three men can make any further scene— if they plan to—the door opens again. I glance back over my shoulder and spot a uniform, a hat, a gun. The tall, slim man with a young face for a man who smells so old tips his hat to the diner owner, eyes never leaving the trio in camo.

"Evening, Dorothy," he says in a cheerful voice. His eyes drift over me then back to the troublemakers. "Boys."

They grunt at him, but seem to unwind. Trouble averted. That is, if Mr. Officer hasn't run my plates. Damn, why didn't I stop to have them switched out before now? One more detail slipped through. I've entirely lost my edge.

A bell dings and Dorothy turns away to the window behind her. Three Styrofoam trays in a plastic bag slide over the counter at me. She winks slowly. "You travel safe now, sweetie."

I nod to her with a smile of my own. "Thanks." The three burly boys don't make it easy to turn and leave, but with the glowering eyes of Dorothy watching and the deputy tipping his hat to me, too, they don't have much choice.

Neanderthals. Any other time, I'd have taken them out back and given them a lesson they would never forget. And would encourage them to treat women with respect from now on. But I have Sage to think about and this cop to avoid.

I breathe a sigh of relief into the night air as I exit,

hurrying to the car. It's not until I pull open the driver's door, I realize something's wrong.

At the exact moment the sound of growling reaches me.

And the door to the diner opens, three heavy sets of footfalls exiting.

The plastic bag hits the driver's seat as I spin, eyes huge, from the empty cabin of the minivan, and spot Sage across the parking lot.

He's standing in front of the jacked-up truck. At a dead white-tailed buck strapped to the hood.

TWENTY

I smell the tang of the dead deer's blood too late, my senses as dulled as my skills. How did I miss the fresh kill? It's a perfect lure for Sage in his state. This can't be happening. Why did I leave him alone? I lurch forward, already running for him, but it's too late. The big men have seen him, are reaching into the back of the truck, pulling out rifles.

I may have to teach them a lesson after all.

"You! Boy!" The one Dorothy called Jake points his shotgun at Sage, but my love ignores him. I can feel Sage's wolf straining against his physical form, wanting to manifest, to rip apart the carcass and feed on it. But Sage is stronger. I siphon him power to keep him stable, but I'm still ten feet from him and he's looking down the barrel of a gun.

A burst of magic-driven speed puts me at Sage's side in time to knock the shotgun away. Whether this man is willing to kill or not, I can't take that chance. Jake's scowl makes him look like a devil disguised in human form. Hate and bitterness and a slew of other human emotions tied to darkness cross the man's face, his friends just as bad.

I know their kind, have encountered them before. Even trained a militia group when it pleased Andre to support their anti-government paranoia. I've had to bring down men like him, hard. And I'm willing to do so again. I do my best to let him see it in my eyes. He doesn't scare me.

Hopefully, that will scare him.

But I can't stay here in a stand-off with three men with guns. There's a deputy inside the diner who can cause me no end of problems if I catch his attention any further. Which means retreat.

"Back off." I glare at Jake, tugging at Sage. "He was just looking."

"He better just be," Jake rumbles, gun coming around again.

Sage fights me, the wolf fights me, but another shot of magic makes him move. I'm now desperate to escape this, spotting the deputy approaching from the diner door.

He glances over Sage and me, coming to a halt as I

continue to fight against the need in Sage's wolf to feed on the carcass. "Put those damned guns down," he says, though he's still looking at me.

"Kid here was messing with our kill." Jake does as he's told, regardless his argument. Considering Sage hadn't touched the deer—well, not yet—his complaint is invalid.

The officer nods to me. "He okay?" He seems nervous, hand on the butt of his gun, other reaching up for the two-way on his shoulder. Please, don't call for backup.

"He's fine." I squash Sage's low growl with more power. There's no way the Enforcers will miss my magic use this time. Werewolves in the US or not, I'm sure there are none in Arizona. And letting out the amount of power I am is as obvious as waving a flag in the air, telling them to come and get me. We have to go. "Thanks, we're leaving."

The three men watch as I drag Sage away, the cop following slowly. I shove my love into the passenger's seat, smothering him with power, turning to find the officer is looking at the plates on the back of the van.

Damn. Damn it all to the deepest hell imaginable. I slip past him, ignoring his eyes as his gaze rises to follow me. I wave a little before slamming the driver's door and gunning the engine.

Sage is devouring the food, the scent no longer

making me hungry, but sick to my stomach. I ignore him, let him gorge his wolf, while I glance back at the diner in my rear view mirror. The cop is talking into his two-way, probably running my plates. Stupid, suspicious, small-town deputy.

Time to dump the van.

I pull over after a mile at the top of a runaway lane built for big rigs, burying it into the woods and scrub as far as I can. Sage is just finishing the last of the meat, fries and buns and condiments scattered everywhere. He looks up at me with regret, coming back to himself, shaking and groaning softly.

"Charlie, I'm sorry."

I leap out of the van and run around the side, jerking the door open and pulling him out with me. He's still in bare feet, dressed in scrubs. No wonder the sight of him set off alarm bells with the deputy. Dumb, Charlotte. Just dumb. This is going to be difficult. And we have no time. The sound of a siren fires off in the distance. The cop is coming and we have to go.

The rumble of a big engine I've heard before is closer and I only recognize it as we plunge into the trees. Sage doesn't complain about his feet, though, and I understand why when I look down. They've changed, transformed into paws, for the best in this situation, but just adding to our troubles. They can't see him like this.

"Run!" I pull him along, feeling him shift beside me,

changing further before returning to human. I drop my shields to support him. It doesn't matter now. Keeping him stable while we run from our pursuers is the only thing I can think about. I'll deal with the Enforcers if they show.

When they show.

The hunters are coming. I catch the scent of the three men on the wind blowing over my shoulder. The siren has fallen quiet, so the cop must be out there, too. But I'm not as worried about him as I am the three giant hunters. Maybe they wouldn't shoot Sage or me in the parking lot of a diner. But these are their woods, their mountains, and if they spot us, if they spot Sage half-turned, I know it will be shoot first and hide the bodies before the deputy can report it.

I glance at my love, the fur bursting from the skin of his arms, the stretching of his muzzle. Like I said, I know their type. If they see Sage change from human to werewolf? He'll have a bullet in his heart before I can do anything to stop it.

We can't run forever. I make a decision, dragging Sage down beside me behind a rock and smother us with power. He fights me, trying to run, and I'm forced to knock him out with magic. As his eyes roll back in his head, I feel the approach of the hunters and know we're out of options.

TWENTY-ONE

My magic slips outward like a net, covering us in mirage. It's one of the first things a werewolf learns to do, to hide their true self from normals. I've taken it one step further, disguising us completely, or as best I can, from human eyes. Though, if they stumble on us physically, we're out of luck.

All this power output will summon the Enforcers, without question. They'll recognize werewolf magic—identify it as my magic with all of this to work with—and investigate. All bets are off on how long it will take them to realize it's me. We can't just sit here.

I shoulder Sage's unconscious body, half-shifting into werewolf form to make the job easier. He groans but falls silent again as I stride through the scrub and up the side of a steep hill. I can't risk taking a trail, I have to make my own. At least my wolf-paw prints won't equate to the sandals I discarded. It should throw the hunter's tracking off if they can't find human feet to follow.

Unless they deduce the girl's feet turned to wolf paws are mine. Then we're in a whole other kind of trouble.

I stumble and almost drop Sage at the sound of voices behind me. They are closer than I expected, this is their territory. Alone, I could outrun them easily. But burdened by Sage, I'm a target. How did they track me? They have to have made the connection.

It's either keep running or stand and fight. And I'm mighty tired of running. A narrow pass at the top of the hill, sided by scrub and a few trees, looks like a great place to make a stand. I slip through it, setting Sage down on the downward slope on the other side, before turning to scan the brush behind me. The three hunters are making their way toward me, guns up and ready. They don't see me, yet, but they are following my wolf tracks.

"Can't be," one hisses. "She's just a girl."

"You saw them footprints shift," Jake snarls back. "Now shut it before she figures out we're here."

"Too late," I say. The three look up with shouts of fear, though I'm in human form. "If you leave now, I'll let you live."

Jake raises his shotgun, hands shaking, eyes huge,

and I know what he's going to say before he says it. "Werewolf."

Damn it. I would have to encounter someone with experience. Still, I have to talk him down if I can. "That's crazy." Even I don't sound convinced. I must work on my acting skills.

All three men quaver, their guns vibrating, aimed at my heart. "Killed one of you lot last year," Jake says, voice steady if his body isn't. "Filthy animals." Fear and fury war in his words. "Bit my brother. Turned him into one of you."

A revenant. Are they being tested here, too? I've heard nothing from the North American Council, but maybe they have no idea.

In a way, it's fortunate these men found it and killed it. On the other hand, I can't help but feel sympathy for the fallen and hatred for Jake and his friends.

"You don't have to do this." I'm surprised how calm my voice is, though this is what I've been raised to do, trained to be. I can take the three of them out easily, my mind tracking a path of attack on autopilot even as I try to talk Jake down. I don't want to have to kill them, despite my disgust. But when I'm faced with guns, death is the most likely outcome.

For them, that is.

Jake's hands shift on the shotgun, just a twitch, but enough for my hyper-alert senses to notice. "I'm going to hang your pretty head in my shed," he says.

His finger tightens on the trigger while my muscles bunch and my wolf surges forward.

The air overhead bursts to life with flashes of blue fire as three Enforcers appear in the night sky. The hunters scream like little girls, staring up into the air for a tortured moment before turning and running back the way they came. I'm clearly the furthest thing from their minds, at this point. Two of the witches in black robes turn and chase the fleeing men, magic pulsing around them, knocking them to the ground. But the third Enforcer lands and walks wearily toward me, his face lined with worry.

"Charlotte." Pender Tremere doesn't threaten me, but I can tell from his posture, he's prepared to take me down if I fight him. I've known Pender as long as I've known Syd. He's always been forced to do the right thing, no matter if that "right" thing goes against true justice. I don't envy him his position or the choices he's been forced to make in the name of witch law. I fear, one day, when he's finally replaced, he will perish within weeks of retiring, unable to bear his guilt any longer. For now, he is an old man in a younger man's body, sad and quiet, but with the same determination I've always felt keeping him here, doing his duty.

"Pender." The feeling is mutual, our duties parallel. I won't let him take me in, take Sage to death. But I don't want to hurt the Enforcer leader, either.

"We're glad you're all right," he says. "We've all been so worried about you." That's Pender. Always kind, with a good heart. If only he would have the courage to step outside the parameters of what he's been told to do. I know better than to argue with him, or try to convince him otherwise. He's lost any spark he gained when helping Syd and Ethpeal to save Miriam from Batsheva and the Council so many years ago. He's been a yes man for far too long to change now.

"Thanks." I am grateful, knowing he cares, despite our opposition. I look over his shoulder at the two Enforcers who are bending over the fallen hunters. "Memory wipes?"

He nods, pushing his hood back. His brown hair is now mostly gray and thinning at the front, face lined and aged beyond his years. The weight of his role hasn't been kind, nor the fact he seems to take everything so personally, as if each incident were his fault, and his alone.

"Will you come quietly?" His voice holds little hope, more pleading than anything. He holds out one hand, trembling slightly, hazel eyes brimming with moisture. He wants me to give in to him, to not make him fight me. But I simply can't.

I shake my head, feel Sage stir behind me. He's in control again, but his wolf is powerful, very powerful, and when he touches my hand, taking it and staring at Pender, I reach out and realize I can tap into Sage's energy.

"You know me better than that, Pender," I say. "Would Syd stand down in the same circumstance?"

The Enforcer leader nods heavily, a tiny smile lifting his thin lips. "I hoped you wouldn't fight me," he says with a tiny, sad smile. "But I do know better. You're more like her than anyone else I've met. Sometimes that's a good thing, Charlotte. But not always." He pauses. "She can't save you, you know. Not from the law. He may not be a witch, but the council agrees with your people. That boy you're traveling with puts us all in danger, and you know it. We have to bring him in."

So he thinks. His words still hurt.

"I'm sorry about this," I say. "Please don't take it personally."

Pender opens his mouth to respond, but I'm not interested in what he has to say. Instead, I draw on Sage even as I gather my own magic and jerk a hole open in the veil.

Sage acts first, as though he expected this, leaping through and pulling me beside him. I leave Pender, open mouthed and staring, power inert as he watches us go, the cut sealing shut behind us.

This time, we have a destination. I'm already focused on Los Angeles, on reaching the city. Still, when the veil tears again, dumping us out, I'm shocked it worked.

I land hard on Sage, hearing him grunt in response to the impact, though he's laughing a moment later as the veil seals shut behind us. The air is warmer here, the tang of salt and pollution strong. I slip from Sage, helping him to his feet, the cold, dirty pavement under my bare skin making me cringe.

"Awesome!" Sage's eyes glow with his wolf for a moment before it retreats. "We made it." He looks around, excitement fading. "This is Los Angeles, right?"

I glance quickly from side to side, assessing our situation. The Enforcers might be able to track us, though I have no idea if they can do so through the veil or not. No sense taking chances. We have to move. The alley we're in is dark, filthy, the walls covered in graffiti, a beaten-up dumpster stinking next to us.

"No idea," I say. "This way." I lead him to the end of the building, looking out into the street. It's run-down, dirty, feels like hopelessness and death. But as I turn and check out the other way, I see the towering high-rises of central Los Angeles in the distance. We did make it. Caine's hometown. I've almost forgotten our end goal in the survival drive getting here. But the focus of our task comes back in a jolt as I hug Sage's arm against me. We're here, and in time, hopefully, to find a cure or at least the sorcerer who made Caine.

I'll wring the information I need from the blood of

anyone who stands in my way.

Exhaustion takes me like a lover, almost knocking my knees out from under me in a wave so powerful I gasp. I wasn't expecting this. But I've pushed myself to my limit, it seems, and I need rest.

We've made it and I'm falling apart.

Sage holds me, concern in his face, his wolf, his scent. "Charlie!"

"I'm okay." It's easy to lie, though I can no longer stand without assistance. The traveling through the veil must have done me in, though he seems to be fine. "But we need help." I hate this weakness. We've come so far, made it to Los Angeles, and I'm a wreck? I won't stand for it. But there's only one person I can call for help who won't make me take Sage back.

Pender said she couldn't help me. I pray he's wrong. I just need a power boost, a little energy to keep me going.

I just hope she's here to answer my call.

I reach for Syd. She's so familiar, her magic, her soul, no matter how little power I have left to search, I know I'll find her if she's on this plane. That's why I'm shocked when another witch's magic touches mine. I flinch back, fearing it's Enforcers. Only to realize I'm wrong.

Charlotte. Tallah Hensley's powerful mind cradles mine. *You made it. Hang tight. I'll be right there.*

TWENTY-TWO

She doesn't give me the option to say no. Her mind is gone again before I can hide from her. I hover with Sage's arms around me, trying to decide what to do, my mind so tired I can barely think.

"Help is coming," I say, "but I'm not sure if it's the help we need."

Sage just shrugs, holding me tight. "We'll figure it out," he says.

Can I trust Tallah? She's the sister of Syd's second, Shenka. Tallah leads the Hensley coven here in California. I forgot she was here, actually, shame on me. And though Tallah held a heavy grudge against Syd for a long time after her sister chose to join the Hayles, Tallah has been quiet and keeping her own council for a long time, now. Ever since her attempt to have witches exposed to normals was shown to be folly, a trick of the Brotherhood.

I know little of her now. But she said nothing about calling the Enforcers. Only that she was coming for me. And that I made it? What does that mean? If she's been expecting me, who told her I was coming?

Piers. Has to be. He's the only one who knows about my plan to come to California. If Piers trusts her... well. We'll have to see.

I'm too tired to run any more. If she can help us, so be it. But if she tries to betray us, to turn us in, I will make certain she suffers for it. For now, I have no choice but to believe she has our best interest at heart. I don't have the power or the energy to do otherwise.

And if she can help...I can't protect Sage from himself alone anymore. That much is obvious. Not from the Enforcers, either, not while trying to solve this mystery and find him a cure. It's just too much for me to do on my own. Someone has to watch him. And maybe Tallah and her people are the help I need.

A terrible thought crosses my mind. I'm less worried about putting the Hensley family in harm's way thanks to my actions than the Hayles. But I'm selfish enough to understand that acceptance. I love Syd and her family and will do everything in my power to keep them safe. But the Hensleys are disposable.

So practical, Charlotte.

We're exposed out here in the street, and exposure puts us at risk. I don't consider normal confrontation until a small pack of young men, mostly Hispanic, have cut us off from behind. A pair of their friends stand in front, knives in hand, covered in tattoos and grinning at me like I'm dinner.

"*Chica*," one says in heavily accented Spanish. "You leave your boyfriend and come be my woman, yeah?" The others laugh as Sage shifts next to me. I find reserves of strength, my wolf responding to the threat of these young men and their little weapons. Sage growls and I feel his wolf rise in response.

"Beat it," I say, stupid to antagonize him, but out of patience. I'm done being chased and threatened and forced to run instead of standing my ground. "And I won't hurt you."

The men groan their good humor at my response. "I like the ones who fight back," he says, two teeth glittering with gold in the streetlight. He makes a rude, sexual gesture with his hands.

Sage's wolf breaks through. "Leave her alone."

The smile vanishes from the gang leader's face. "You dead, bro."

This punk has no idea. If Sage turns, they are lost. I push my love back with one hand on his chest. "Sage," I whisper. "Keep it together."

He swallows hard, but his wolf still fights for

freedom. Mine would love nothing more than to show these stupid boys the error of their ways. But I can't let Sage turn. Not after everything we've been through.

A car screeches to a halt and three people leap out, a second—a huge SUV—stuttering on giant tires. Magic flies, the gang suddenly frozen in blue fire.

Tallah emerges from the black truck, waving to me. "Hurry! We can't hold them for long without Enforcers noticing."

I hesitate. If I do this, if I lead Sage into her hands, we're stuck. She has a whole coven of power to use against us. Can I take that risk?

"Charlotte." She must feel my tension because she reaches for me with power, gentle, supportive. "I would have already turned you in if I was going to."

Time to take a chance. Sage and I run for her while her witches carefully manipulate the gang's memory. We're in the SUV and driving off, the second car on our heels, before the leader can even turn around to watch us go.

I sink back into the leather seat, catch Tallah's eyes in the rearview mirror. The last of my strength runs out of me as her mind softly lulls me to sleep.

Sunlight wakes me, warming my face, the thin, silk sheets over my body. I stretch, turning to Sage sleeping beside me. His bare chest feels amazing on my cheek, the scent of him full, rich, a wolf's smell.

I sit up suddenly, looking down at him. His left shoulder is wrapped in fresh bandages, but he looks peaceful enough, and feels it, too. Robust, almost, as though he's more than he's ever been. Can this bite turn out to be a good thing? I can only hope that's the case.

My gaze turns to the bank of glass doors looking out over the beach, the ocean in the near distance, flimsy curtains wafting on a soft breeze coming through one half-open panel. The king-sized bed is soft and comfortable, but I'm hyper-aware now of time and its passing and I have only one day left to find a cure for Sage before it's too late.

I slip from bed, pad across the room. A huge bathroom waits, marble everything, a giant glass shower beckoning. I give in though I don't really have the time, closing the door behind me to block the sound from Sage, standing under the hot water for a full ten minutes, trying to absorb it directly through my skin. A nice scrubbing with some lovely soap and my hair clean and soft from the conditioner Tallah supplied and I'm ready to face the world.

Clean clothes wait in the bedroom, piled on the chair by the door. I pull on a pair of shorts and new underwear, such a relief. The matching bra is cute enough I know Tallah understands my full relationship to Sage. A T-shirt and sandals complete my new look. I quietly slip from the room, leaving Sage still sleeping peacefully. He's earned it and I need to confront Tallah without him to find out what her plan is.

As I make my way through the house, memories surface. Of spending a vacation here with Syd after her first year at Harvard. At least I know where to go, the lay of the land. And though my nerves are still raw, I feel less concerned as I go, knowing we've been here in Tallah's care for hours without any sign of Enforcers. She was correct. If she were going to turn us in, she would have done so long ago.

So what is her stake in this?

The wide-open living and dining area, capped by a massive kitchen in the open-concept central room, fills with the scent of the ocean, the doors open wide, a soft breeze carrying fresh air through the house. I pause at the entry, at the sight of Tallah and another woman sitting on a cream sofa looking out over the beach. She looks up, spots me, gestures me closer with a warm smile, and I walk toward her, hovering at the edge of the carpet marking the living room.

"Charlotte." Tallah rises, comes to me, hugs me, and I hug her back. "We're so happy to see you're safe."

That sounds familiar. Pender's words, paraphrased. I nod. "Thanks for the rescue."

She shakes her head with a laugh, leading me to the couch. The woman with her rises to make space for me.

"Not at all," she says. "I'm sure you would have managed on your own without me. I'm just happy to help." She points to the slender woman who smiles at me, her brown eyes and dark skin capped with a tight round of spiral black curls. "This is Anna Mosely," she says. "My second."

"It's a pleasure to see you again," Anna says. "We met when you and Syd visited years ago."

I shake her hand out of politeness before turning to Tallah. "We can't stay here."

Tallah doesn't respond to my statement, instead gesturing at the kitchen. "Let me offer you breakfast. Coffee?"

My teeth grind together in frustration. But her offer makes my stomach rumble and I nod in acceptance. Anna bustles off to the kitchen and starts cooking while I pace the front of the open doors.

"I understand there's a time limit," Tallah says, coming to stop me from my endless walk. "Seven days?"

She's been talking to someone, all right, and maybe not just Piers. "Femke?"

Tallah nods. "We've all been keeping an eye open for you," she says. "Outside the usual channels." She winks slowly. So my friends have been looking out for me. Tears sting my eyes in a rush of gratitude.

"Thank you," I whisper, voice thick.

Tallah's hand settles on my arm. "Anything for you,

Charlotte. Anything." She lets me go, sits back, dark eyes unreadable. "Now," she says. "Tell me of this cure you're looking for."

I choke on an answer. "There has to be one," I say. Such a silly thing to cling to, faced with the bright sunshine and reality. I've been telling myself the same for days now, that there must be a way to reverse this. But now, sitting here in her kitchen, faced with the new day in her presence, I find my certainty waning.

"I'm not doubting you," she says, though my own grows now like a sickly cancer in my heart. "Piers told me about Lula and Phon, how they tried to heal Sage from the beginning." She glances at Anna who nods. "And we had a look ourselves, after we brought you in." Tallah frowns, long-fingered hands steepling before her in an elegant triangle. "It should be possible." She seems frustrated. "Though I fear it will take a sorcerer to do it."

"Piers tried." I almost cry the words.

Tallah leans forward and squeezes my hand with her strong fingers. "I know," she says. "But even he seems to think one versed in the creation of werewolves would be able to make a difference." He didn't tell me that. A stab of anger is chased off by annoyance at myself. It's not like he had a great deal of time to do so. "The question is," Tallah goes on, "are we already out of time?"

I shiver but nod slowly. "I don't know," I whisper, as though speaking up will make what I say true. "It's possible the infection has already traveled too far, changed him too much." He carries a wolf in him now. Will it be possible to strip that away?

Tallah wrinkles her nose, letting my hand go. "Infection is such a dirty word," she says. "He's changing, Charlotte. But he's not sick."

"He doesn't feel like a revenant," I say. "I don't know what he's becoming."

She taps her nails on the side of her coffee cup, the breeze ruffling her sleek, black hair, sun warming her dark cheek with its light. "Your race were all revenants once," she says, making my hackles rise, stirring my anger even as she waves off my reaction. "You know what I mean." Her apology is in her tone, though my rage vanishes as I realize I've had this conversation before, in Ukraine, with a cigar-smoking man who helped me when no one else would. Iosif said the same thing, didn't he?

"We were created in the beginning," I say. "But only those born are real werewolves."

"Says who?" Anna cuts in, though she blushes and smiles a little at her own boldness.

"Says the law." I shake my head.

"And who created that law?" Tallah's eyes narrow, watching me carefully.

It hits me with the force of a punch to the gut. "The Black Souls," I say.

They made our laws, all of them, enforced them for

centuries. Created us and our doctrine from whole cloth and left us to reinforce those laws among ourselves while punishing those who broke them with death.

"But those laws exist for good reason." I hate to defend the word of the sorcerers who made us, but it's true. Revenants must be killed before they infect others.

"Maybe they did," Tallah stresses the last word. "But do they stand now, Charlotte? So much has changed for your people since Syd freed you. Has anyone reexamined the laws that govern you in this new context?" She pauses, sipping her coffee. "How exactly has your freedom from their taint changed you?"

I stare at her, mouth watering, stomach heaving. I have no idea how to answer her.

The tension in me breaks as I feel him enter, turning to see Sage join us. He's dressed in fresh clothes, too, T-shirt and shorts, and looks far calmer than I feel. I can't help but stare at him as he crosses toward me, Tallah and Anna's questions circling in my head. What is Sage? And could it be the laws demanding his death are no longer necessary?

But no, the other revenants, the ones in Europe…I'm so confused, my heart pounding, the entirety of what I was raised to believe a mushy mess in my head.

Sage joins me without a clue to my state, sitting between Tallah and me after brief introductions, devouring the giant plate of sausage and pancakes Anna places before him. She continues to cook as I force myself to finish my meal. Anna's eyes widen as Sage just goes on eating.

"Your appetite will level off eventually," I say. And stop myself. Since when did I start thinking of Sage as a werewolf? He has the appetite of a pubescent, their voraciousness legendary. But he's not, he's a revenant. This isn't going to be permanent. And yet, the conversation I just had, the memory of the one in Ukraine with Iosif, makes me pause again.

He grins at me around a slice of toast, no clue what's going on in my aching head. "Hope so," he says.

I turn then to Tallah and ask her, point blank, what I need to know. "The Enforcers?"

She sighs, sets her coffee down. "I'm not fully in line with the Council's plans these days." Her frown, mirrored by Anna's, makes me nervous. What's happening? Should I know about it? Does Syd? I shake off those questions. Not only am I not Syd's bodywere any longer, I have other things to worry about.

Tallah goes on. "I've been ordered to turn you over," she says, "if you're spotted by my family." Her nose wrinkles again, an adorable affectation. "You must know the North American Council has decided to cooperate with the demands of the werenation that you be returned to them for punishment."

I knew this already, but hearing her say it still freezes me in place, breath catching in my chest. Even Sage stops mid-bite. Until Tallah smiles at me.

"Silly," she says. "In case you haven't figured things out already, I've decided," she returns to her coffee with a casual air, "to ignore that order. You're both safe with me."

TWENTY-THREE

I tell Tallah everything I can remember, doing my best to order my thoughts, wandering from time to time, though Sage is wonderful at bringing me back. So much has happened in the last week, I can barely believe it's only been such a short stretch.

When I touch on the Rupe sighting and my worries about the Brotherhood, Tallah mirrors my concern.

"We've been careful as a council to watch for any appearances of the Brotherhood and Belaisle," she says, leaning toward me, coffee long cold and forgotten by her elbow. "I'll be very disappointed in myself if we've missed their return."

"Considering their slippery nature," I say, "it's hardly your fault, Tallah."

She just shakes her head. "Have you seen Liander

himself?"

It's my turn to for denial. "Just Rupe," I say. "Though there are sorcerers at work here, that much is obvious." Isabelle's problems with tracking Sage tell me that much.

Tallah is frowning, though not in anger. "It's possible Rupe is working on his own, then," she says. "If Liander hasn't made himself known."

I find that idea highly unlikely, but I can't discount it. "Maybe," I say, knowing I sound dubious.

Tallah reaches forward and squeezes my hand. "I'm not doubting you," she says, "or minimizing your concern. Not in the least. In fact, I'm even more worried now. If Rupe is working with Belaisle and the Brotherhood, this is a good thing." She pulls back, tight grin growing on her lovely face. "With warning they've risen, we can do more to pin them down."

"But if Rupe is on his own?" I see the complication possibilities even as Tallah speaks.

"That means he's branched off," the coven leader says, returning to grim unhappiness. "And we have a different batch of sorcerers to worry about."

"I want to know why he tried to kidnap me." Sage leans into me. "In the hospital."

"That's the biggest question of all." I focus on Tallah. "If Rupe is able to make revenants like Caine and his pack, then why is he creating disasters and scattering them around northern Europe?" That same query has haunted me for days.

Tallah nods slowly. "I think you're building an excellent case against Rupe working with the Brotherhood," she says. I frown at her, but hold my tongue as she goes on. She looks distant, as though her mind is elsewhere, but she continues to speak so I let her work it out without interruption. "If Rupe is making revenants, in line with the Brotherhood, that suggests Belaisle is part of the process." She snaps her fingers. "But if Rupe is on his own, it explains the mess he's making in Europe, doesn't it?"

I shake my head. "I'm not sure I follow."

Tallah grins, shrugs. "Sorry," she says. "Shenka used to tease me about my mental leaps." She focuses on me with a tense smile. "Here's where my head went. Rupe used to work with Belaisle, we know that for certain." I nod while Sage prods me.

"Who?" He looks back and forth between us.

I almost shush him, but he frowns at me.

"This is my life we're talking about," he says. "I think I deserve to know the full story. At least enough to follow along and not feel like an idiot."

I squeeze his hand in sudden regret. "I'm sorry," I say. "Liander Belaisle is the leader—or was—of a group of sorcerers."

Sage nods. "The Brotherhood."

Tallah salutes him with her mug. "Correct," she says. "And his henchman is—"

"Rupe," Sage says, now grinning himself.

"Also correct," Tallah says. "A young and troublesome sorcerer who betrayed Syd, I believe."

I shrug off that comment. "Go on," I say.

Sage looks like he wants to protest and I know he has little information, but there will, hopefully, be lots of time later to fill him in. Tallah looks back and forth between us before refilling her coffee cup.

"So, Rupe's allegiance is to Belaisle," Tallah says. "Or was when Syd defeated him at the battle at the stronghold." Sage opens his mouth but I stomp on his foot and he goes silent with a frown of irritation.

"Exactly," I say. "So what are you thinking?"

"There's nothing to say Rupe still works for Belaisle," Tallah says. "In fact, it's possible the whole Brotherhood did fall apart after the defeat." Masses of sorcerers abandoned the cause, it's true, though I never fully trusted their exodus. "Rupe might have been Belaisle's boy in the beginning, but if things went south, what's to say Rupe didn't decide to cut his losses and make his own way?"

I nod. "All right," I say. "I'll buy that."

Anna rolls her eyes as she rejoins us. "Thousands wouldn't," she says as she winks at her leader.

Tallah softly smacks her arm. "I'm eternally tortured

for my musings," she says. "So this is the final piece, then, Charlotte. What if it was Belaisle who created Caine and his pack?" Her eyes lift to mine, shifting out of glee and into speculation. She snaps her fingers at me. "After Rupe jumped ship?"

I stare at her as my mind churns.

"Consider this," Tallah says. "Belaisle is weak and has lost control of his people. He needs some kind of army or something to rebuild his base of power." Tallah's dark eyes glisten as she races on. "He figures out how to make werewolves again. Maybe he finds the process the Black Souls used, or maybe he makes it up himself." Her coffee sloshes as her excitement rises. "He's had lots of time to work things out, hasn't he? Years now."

My stomach wants to reject the breakfast I've eaten. "A new master," I say.

She shrugs. "Not for your people," Tallah says. "You're already free." I try to accept that so my mind won't explode in worry. "But for a new breed of werewolves, it's possible. More than possible. Highly likely."

"So you're saying this Rupe fellow stole the idea from his former boss?" Sage is clearly listening better than I am.

Tallah nods enthusiastically. "Precisely," she says. "It makes total sense. The revenants in Europe—"

"And here," I say, remembering the hunters in

Arizona.

Tallah pales, dark skin ashen a moment. "First I heard," she says.

I wave her on.

She does so, with less passion. "All his attempt to recreate what Belaisle did."

"Where did he get what he needed to start the process?" Sage looks at me with open curiosity while my heart bleeds.

"He must have kidnapped a werewolf," Tallah and I say at exactly the same time. She nods. "One bite from a full-born werewolf to a normal creates a revenant."

Sage doesn't comment again, so Tallah goes on. "He figures it out through trial and error, ends up with Caine and his pack. They're not perfect, since you said you can still sense revenant on them, but they are functional and have magic."

I nod. "Sorcery," I say. "He has to have tapped into their innate sorcery and used it to transform them, triggering the elemental magicks other werewolves use." Fire and earth, namely.

Tallah's hands skim over the smooth surface of the table, palms down. "But he abandons the project, for whatever reason, and Rupe in the process."

But why? We have less information than I would like to be speculating like this, and no proof whatsoever Tallah is right.

Tallah seems to agree with me, her frown returning. "I wish we knew more," she says. "But there has to be a reason Rupe is on his own, if he's splintered free of Belaisle."

"Maybe an internal division?" Sage shrugs as we stare at him. "Happens all the time in big business. People branch off and start their own thing, right?"

The only way I can see Belaisle would let Rupe go is if the younger sorcerer killed him. Not an unpleasant thought. I've never wished such ill on anyone as I do Liander Belaisle. Except for Andre Dumont.

"Okay, so here's Rupe, young and ambitious," Tallah says, excitement of the story rising in her eyes, "decides to stick it to Belaisle and take his handful of buddies elsewhere to plot world domination or whatever else he has in mind."

I'm following her. "He realizes he needs an army himself," I say, "especially if he finds out Belaisle is building one. A controllable force if he's going to defeat his enemies. Or take control from Belaisle."

Tallah grins. "Exactly. And what better model than the werewolves?"

What better model, indeed.

"Only one problem," Tallah says. "He knows Belaisle has done it, made revenants who aren't insane. But he doesn't know how his former leader accomplished it."

"Which is why he's experimenting," I say, nodding. "But is he working with Caine and the others?"

"Possibly," Tallah says. "This smacks of Belaisle disappearing, going missing." She's hesitant, but continues her line of thought. "It could be Rupe has already killed him and taken over the Brotherhood. Which means Caine and his pack are now loyal to Rupe by default."

I can't imagine someone as wily as Belaisle falling to someone like Rupe. But odder things have happened.

Tallah sits back with a sigh. "This is all well and good, in theory," she says, "but without proof, we're singing in the wind."

I nod, glum all over again. "What about the Steam Union?" Didn't Piers say there was a branch here in California? Maybe they can help where my friend's branch won't. He's already told me as much. But an independent group might be more pliable.

Tallah doesn't look optimistic. "We've been trying to contact them," she says. "We know they are here. But they run from us every time we get close and refuse to connect." She shrugs. "Piers has been trying to help us. In fact, that's how we knew to keep an eye out for you. He told me you were heading this way."

I knew it. My guilt about him and his part in this makes me sad. "Is he in much trouble?"

Tallah laughs. "Don't worry about Piers Southway,"

she says. "He's in hot water with his mother and Femke, but you know he'll come out the other side smelling like a rose."

I allowed her good humor to ease my conscience. "And werewolves?" Surely, she and her coven heard hints of a pack here. "Are there any in the area?" It would take me some time to cover enough ground to find hints of others like me.

Anna looks uncomfortable. "We thought so," she says. "About two years ago. They showed up out of the blue and then they were gone. So fast I doubted they were here at all."

Tallah pats her hand. "We went looking, thinking they might be some of your family trying to relocate, wanted to make them feel welcome. But we couldn't find a trace."

"That has to be Caine's pack." Now I'm excited.

She nods. "I can only assume that's the case."

"Which means," I say, "if Belaisle was the one who created Caine and his pack, he is—or was—here in California." And he's the sorcerer I need to find to gain the cure for Sage. Now there's a troubling thought. What if Tallah is right and Rupe really has killed his former master? That would mean no cure since, so far, Rupe has been unable to make revenants who don't devolve.

"And that Rupe wants Sage because he's the first successful new werewolf he's created," Tallah says.

That shuts us all up. I listen to the breeze, the call of sea birds through the open door and try to figure out what to do next. "Can you tell me where the pack was supposed to hold territory?"

Anna nods quickly. "Of course," she says. "But there's more."

Tallah grimaces. "We don't know if this is connected," she says, as if it's an old argument.

"With all we've discovered and posited," Anna says, "it makes sense, Tal."

Tallah nods. "Go ahead."

I lean in, Sage at my side, as Anna speaks.

"Just prior to the werewolf pack appearing," she says, "there was a string of missing person reports. Mostly from the street community, but more widespread than anything Los Angeles has ever seen."

"You think they might have been test subjects?" I shudder at Sage's casual question.

"Possibly," Anna says. "And then, an entire biker gang disappeared. It was huge news, because the leader was well-known and feared in the community."

"Do you have a photo?" If it's who I hope it is, we have proof. She holds out her hands, projecting a holographic image of a newspaper front page. The LA Times shows me the grinning, arrogant face of Cicero Caine.

Sage speaks up before I can. "That's him." He's

paled, hand going to his shoulder on reflex.

"So, now we know," Tallah says. "You have proof he was human."

He changed his name, took his whole gang with him, turned to werewolf revenants.

"We have to get this information to my grandfather." Oleksander wants proof. Now he has it. That part of my task is done. I still have a cure to find—if there is one—but at least my grandfather will be able to move against Caine and his pack.

Tallah turns to Anna who closes her hands, shutting off the hologram. "I'll make sure Oleksander has this information immediately," she says. "And with pleasure."

TWENTY-FOUR

Tallah has just finished speaking when the air beside me ripples, turns black. I leap to my feet, but not out of fear. The moment Piers strides through, I throw myself into his arms and hug him to me.

"You idiot," I whisper in his ear before leaning back and hitting him hard in the shoulder. He rolls with the punch, letting out a squeak of protest while I hug him again. "What are you doing here?"

Piers grins at me when I finally let him go. "Figured I'm in enough trouble already, a little more won't make much difference." He raises his gray eyes to wink at Tallah and Anna. "Ladies." His tall body bends in a half bow. They both wave a little while he turns to Sage. His eyes tighten around the corners, but his ever-present grin remains. "Wolf boy."

Sage snarls, but when I turn, I see the startled look on his face. His wolf reacts before he can stop it. "Piers," Sage says, far more civil than his previous greeting.

Wait, Piers is here. We've been down this road before, and with dangerous results. "Your mother will track you here." I spin back on him, panic returning. "You have to go." I don't want him to leave. Having people around who care, who understand, it feels like being part of a pack again. But if his presence will bring Enforcers, I have to send him away.

"She won't," he says, grim bitterness flaring a moment before it disappears behind his enigmatic smile. "In fact, I've seen to it my mother will never again be able to use me against anyone. Ever."

I stare in shock. "What are you talking about?" He's Steam Union. She's his leader. There's no alternative to doing her ultimate bidding. Unless. Oh, Piers.

"You see," he says, booping me on the nose with one thin finger, "I've made a life decision, a change of fate, if you will." His grand delivery of his lines could come from a well-practiced play. A tragedy, though he tries for comedy. "After a brief, yet enlightening, conversation with dear Mummy, I've chosen to cut myself off from the Steam Union and sever my association once and for all."

"You what?" Another punch finds his shoulder, this

one without power behind it, my strength stolen by my shock. "You're insane." The Steam Union is his life.

"No," he says, "disillusioned and unwilling to follow a stubborn leader who can't see past her fears and self-centered need to control everything." He tosses his white-blond hair, the ponytail bouncing over his shoulder. "About time I left," he adds with an arrogant sniff. "I've long railed against the narrow-minded ways of the Steam Union. Just ask Syd." He winks at me, though there is pain far behind his eyes. This has cost him far more than he's willing to admit. "Thanks to my mother's unwillingness to listen to reason yet again, I could follow no other course of action but to release myself from her influence."

"I bet that made her happy." Eva Southway isn't the kind of woman you cross without consequences.

He shrugs. "Her satisfaction with the way things have turned out is not my concern." He stretches, draws a big breath of air he lets out in a happy gust, still playing his part. "So this is what freedom feels like. Remarkable. Should have tried it years ago." He nudges me. "Highly recommend it."

Tallah's shock slips into sad humor. "Piers," she says. "What will you do?"

His shoulders hunch before he sighs, dropping the act. "Look, I know I'm making light of my choice. But it really was inevitable. I can't live like that anymore. My mother is a tyrant, and if being a part of the Steam Union means being inflexible and turning in my friends, I won't do it." He waggles his eyebrows at the Hensley leader. "Besides, I have a coven leader or two who might be willing to take me in if I make my case." The faintest hint of pleading is in his voice, though I doubt Tallah hears it. My ears are just sensitive, especially to Piers.

Tallah nods, smiling for real this time. "We would be honored to have you."

Piers sweeps into another bow. "Delightful. Now, let's talk compensation." His eyes narrow, hands rubbing together, making Tallah laugh.

I hug him again, shattering his little show. "You did this for me." No matter how hard I try, I keep dragging the people I care about into trouble over a choice I made. Piers's defection is my fault, no matter what he says.

He shakes his head, laughing with the bitterness returned. "Don't flatter yourself, princess," he says, tone softer and kinder than his words. "I did this for purely selfish reasons." He steps away from me, winking as his old charm returns. "Now, tell me we have a plan. I'm all in, regardless. The madder the better, in my opinion."

Anna pours him a cup of coffee while Tallah tells him what we've deduced. I sit with Sage, holding his hand, listening and processing. Piers might be trying to protect me from guilt, but part of his choice is my fault. And I'll never forget his sacrifice.

"Track down the creator, check." Piers nods. "And track the Steam Union pocket, check. Perhaps find ourselves some Brotherhood traitors and wring information from them. Most excellent. Timeline?"

I glance at Sage. "A day," I say. "At the most."

Sage meets my eyes, his calm despite what has to be a frustrating conversation going on around him. "I feel fine, you know," he says. "Since San Antonio, when the antibiotics kicked in."

I don't say anything, unable to speak.

Sage turns to smile at the others. "Whatever's coming," he says, "I'm not afraid. I think Tallah is right. Whoever made me, they figured it out." He flexes his shoulder. "It's weird and everything, but I've never felt stronger. Or more myself." He squeezes my hand as if to reassure me. Like he should be thinking about me at all, considering. "It's going to be okay, Charlie. I can feel it."

I wish I shared his optimism. Instead, I wrap myself in the pride and duty of my people to keep from crying and close myself off from him. He must feel it, because he releases my hand and looks down, falling silent again.

Doesn't he know we can't afford to think in terms of hope right now? We have too much yet to come to fall into that trap. I know Syd would chide me for my negativity. She thrives on hope to carry her through conflict after conflict. But I was raised differently.

Piers meets my eyes "I think we're all aware you're

not a real revenant," he says. Tallah nods, Anna's face creased in a sad but supportive smile. "While I adore Charlotte and would do anything for her, you're another matter." Sage's head snaps up, frown tight and dark. "If I thought for one second you were about to turn into a slavering psychopath, I'd kill you myself and her wants be damned." I'm scowling now, too.

"I wouldn't risk my coven," Tallah says with a gentle smile, "if I thought otherwise myself." She folds her napkin between her fingers. "I won't lie to you, Sage. This is a huge risk. But I believe you are evolving into something important." Her dark eyes glisten with blue magic a moment. "I've felt your spirit. There is nothing in you that tells me you are a risk. To the contrary." She gestures to me. "You feel more a werewolf than Charlotte does, whatever that means."

I gape at her while Piers snorts.

"Same here," he says, gray eyes sparkling. "Seriously, Charlotte. You thought I'd take your side and throw away everything if I didn't think he was valuable?"

I shake my head. "You could have told me sooner." Is it true? Have I been watching for the darkness for so long I missed the light in Sage? I feel for him, but he's the same. Isn't he?

Sage visibly releases his anger. "Thank you," he says to Tallah, ignoring Piers. "Your help means a lot to me."

Tallah pats his hand. "We'll figure this out," she

says. "No matter what that means." She winks at me. "And maybe change some laws along the way to include a new evolution of werewolf."

Piers rolls his eyes as I ponder the possibility. Is Sage what we as a nation are meant to become? If so, how can I prove it?

"Anything else?" The blond sorcerer crosses his arms over his chest as though bored with our conversation.

No one speaks further. The tasks ahead are enough.

"All right," Piers climbs to his feet, his discarded longcoat left on the back of the chair as he rolls up the sleeves of his button-up, exposing pale, wiry arms. "Leave the Steam Union to me. I've played Mr. Nice Piers all along, let them have their cat and mouse moments. Whatever it is they fear, I'll give them something to be afraid of." He grins at me, clearly enjoying himself. "I've been waiting for this moment, you have no idea. Didn't have permission before. Coven Leader?" He turns to her, expectant.

Tallah smiles. "Permission granted. Though consider yourself a free agent with ties to the family, Piers. I'm not your mother."

"My dear lady," he says. "You certainly aren't, being a witch of action." Now I don't feel so bad. He truly seems enthusiastic about the whole thing. Perhaps this is a gift, the push he needed to shed his domineering mother and her antiquated ways. I know the feeling. "Now, if you'll excuse me. It's time to start throwing my weight around and see what shakes loose."

"Can I ask a question?" Sage's hand tightens on mine, warm to the point of uncomfortable, though I refuse to let go. "Does this mean I'm going to be okay?"

We all stare at him while he looks around, trying to gauge an answer from our faces.

"Caine and his people," Sage says. "They are normal. Well," he laughs, "normal-ish. I have a feeling they were pretty badass and a little nuts before they were turned into werewolves."

I have to agree with him there. "So you're wondering if you'll turn out like them?" I sniff him, relieved there's still no sign of revenant taint and that the scent of the secondary infection is long faded. My wolf chuffs over the idea he could be much more than I ever considered. "I don't know, Sage. None of us do. But it makes sense that if you are the next incarnation, that if Rupe figured out what Belaisle missed, it's the reason he wants you back."

"So he can copy what he did with you," Tallah says, voice soft. "Study you to see what worked and why."

I nod. "Which means it's possible you will be okay." Can I really bring myself to believe that?

Sage sighs, smiles a little. "But it's also possible I could devolve into a slavering monster at a moment's notice."

I doubt that very much after everything Tallah and Piers have said. There's something more at work here, something I'm not seeing, maybe not willing to see. If Sage is our next evolution, he still feels incomplete, like his wolf has other plans.

Piers breaks the silence by slapping Sage firmly on the shoulder. Sage winces, reaching for it while I glare at my sorcerer friend.

"Fear not," Piers says in his cheery British voice, "if you do, we'll make sure you have a grand exit."

"I'd rather find a cure." I glare at Piers who winks.

Sage turns to look at me. "I already told you," he says. "If it comes down to it, I want to be a werewolf."

Tallah clears her throat, Anna rising quickly, taking coffee cups away. They sense the sudden intimacy, though Piers hovers, watching, hurt in his eyes while his lips continue to smile.

"You can't," I say. Why doesn't he understand? I should have had this conversation with him long ago, but the timing was always terrible and hope seemed the brighter choice. Now I see my folly. He's really deluding himself. "They'll kill you." My people. Whether he's okay or not.

"The laws can change," Sage says. "We'll make them change. But I'm going to be a werewolf, Charlotte. I'm staying with you."

TWENTY-FIVE

I rise from the table, pulling Sage aside, out the door and onto the deck for a private talk, or as private as we're going to get. Piers stays behind, though from the belligerent frown he gives me as I glance back, he would rather follow and maybe do something permanent to make Sage go away forever.

This independent streak of his seems to have triggered more than I expected.

Sage is just as stiff as my sorcerer friend, anger in his face, his stance, the scent of him as his wolf argues without speaking.

"I thought you understood," I say, keeping my voice low. "But now I know I've failed to explain clearly. That's my fault." My chest heaves in a sigh, heart hurting as I think of him and his family, waiting for him to visit at

Christmas, loving their son, their brother, just the way he is. My own selfish need wishes Sage and I could be together, but I have to put him first. Which means encouraging him to return to human, if possible. "I let you hold your hope, Sage, knowing it kept you going. But you have to listen to me now. You have to believe me." I shake my black bob, not wanting to be angry, but not knowing how else to feel. Not angry with him but at the laws and rules and old fools that will keep us apart. "No matter what happens here, Sage, the pack will never accept you. Live and be a werewolf or die as a monster, you're a revenant, not born to our people. And that is a truth no one can change." Unless Rupe and Belaisle have altered the rules with their meddling. What does that mean for the werenation?

"And you're a princess," he says. "I get it. I heard you the first time, in my cell, when I was waiting to die. I know what you told me. I've been thinking about it ever since." He's not emotional, in fact he's more calm and convincing than I am. "But times change, Charlie. Your race has gone through a huge shift, thanks to Syd. At least from what you told me. You've gained your freedom. And that freedom should come with the chance to do things differently, to assess every opportunity, every following change, with fresh eyes." How very reasonable. He should have been a lawyer, a diplomat. What a wereking he would make.

Stop it, Charlotte.

"You need a lesson in werelaw," I say, a soft shake in my voice. "Also my fault." I draw a breath. "No werewolf shall ever make another through their bite. Such an act will mean the instant death of the were who bit the human and the execution of the revenant upon first manifestation of infection. Without fail, without mercy, that is the law." And has been since we were made.

He wrings his hands, showing distress, though his face remains calm. "I'm so foreign to all this, but I do know one thing. I love you. I will die for you, or live outside pack law if that's what I need to do. But if I'm not going to turn into a monster, if I'm some new creature outside your expectations, I want to explore that. Figure out what being the new me means." He pauses. "I know you think I might shift and implode or something at any point. But, Charlotte, I feel amazing. I've never felt so strong, so stable in my entire life." He drops his hands. "I've spent most of my life learning to fight so I'll never have to, looking for a way to feel powerful." Sage looks away, at the ocean. "You're not the only one with a dark past." When he meets my eyes again, his are full of wonder. "This wolf inside, growing with me, is changing me. For the better. I just know it."

Misery wars with need and hunger for him. "Sage."

He cuts me off with the wave of one hand. "Please, listen. I'm not going to give up on us. As long as I'm here, inside here," he taps his chest, "and the wolf lets me, I'm going to hang onto the hope you and I can be together forever, the way I've always wanted. I promise, if you want that, too, nothing is going to keep me from you."

How can I hurt him after he's bared his soul to me? But I can't allow him to carry false hope. No more than I can. I'm here to save his life, but that's it. That's all it can be. I tremble inside, knowing I'm lying to myself, that I want to embrace what he's offered me, more than anything, my mind whirling with ways I can say yes. I could spend the rest of my life hiding with him, create our own little pack, staying under the radar. It would mean sacrifice for him, for his family...

His family.

Which is why I prepare to say no.

"Even if," I say, "you prove to be a perfect revenant, a new werewolf in full control of his power, and even if," I stress those words for the second time, "the werenation lets you live, no matter how this turns out, we will never be permitted to mate, to be together, to create offspring. Our people's freedom is just too young." Far too young. So much fear still exists. Oleksander is proof of that. "You will be a pariah, segregated from the pack, a lone wolf on your own. Do you understand what that means?"

He nods. "I do."

"No," I snarl. "You don't. Werewolves are pack creatures, Sage. We need each other." Memories of childhood, of loneliness and loss, haunt me. How the Dumonts separated me from the others, kept me out of touch with my little pack. The way it burned in the back of my mind, drove me almost to the brink of insanity, as bad as the physical torture Andre inflicted. "A cure is a better choice. So you can live out your life as a human."

Sage's calm hasn't shifted, though cold bitterness joins it now. "You'd let that happen to me."

I throw my hands up in the air. "I would have no choice," I say. "I'm the heir to the throne of the werenation. My people's needs come before my own." I turn my back on him, hugging myself, hating myself. "I've already broken so many of our laws, turned away from my people in an effort to save you. Were I to go against pack will and try to integrate you, it would cause such a rift in my people I don't know what the result would be." I spin on him, putting all of my pain and fear and love in my eyes. "Please understand, I love you, Sage. But they are my people and I must put them first."

If I ever get a chance. I've been thinking all along Oleksander will ensure I am chained to the throne after this. But there's a distinct possibility he will be forced to rule against me instead. The outcome could be much more permanent. Sage may yet survive, while I could be tried and killed for betraying my people and never sit on the throne of the werenation. Even if he is cleared, there is a chance my life will either be over, or I will be enslaved, mated to the were of the people's choice, for the express purpose of producing offspring for the throne.

Sage doesn't need to hear that now. I'm done arguing with him. He will be safe and human or protected from the pack and a werewolf, but those are his only two options. End of story.

Why can't he understand that?

I leave him there on the deck, going back inside, heart breaking. Maybe we could run away, be fugitives forever. But I can't bring myself to fully turn away from my people, not when threats like Rupe and Caine hover over what we've struggled to build.

The room is empty, all but for Tallah. She waits for me with sad eyes, reaches out to me. I go to her, hug her as she whispers in my ear. "It's not easy being a leader."

I pull away, wiping at a tear that managed to escape. "Syd taught me nothing is impossible," I say. "But sometimes it really feels like she's wrong."

"Trust her," Tallah says with a smile. "You know none of us will ever let anything happen to you. Not if you let us help." She hesitates. "I know your people are tied to their laws. And how hard it is to change those laws. But you have powerful leaders on your side. Is it possible something could be done?"

Not her, too. "I wish," I say.

She shrugs, sorrow on her beautiful face. "You would know better than I," she says. "But it seems to me part of being a leader is showing your people the future is now, and that change is a good thing that will bring them prosperity."

My heart skips. "Maybe if I hadn't betrayed them by running off with Sage."

"Or," she says, drawing out the word with a twinkle in her eye, "you instead departed, as was your duty, to investigate Caine and his people, using the revenant as a guide to their home base, thus uncovering a sorcerer plot to again enslave your people, and saving them all from a terrible fate."

It's impossible not to laugh. "A nice story," I say.

"One with merit." She grips my arms in her hands, staring me down with her dark eyes. "Charlotte, I know the world looks black and white sometimes. But shades of gray go a long way to nudging life into the path you want it to go."

I kiss her cheek as a light bulb goes off. She's totally right. I've been thinking in terms of a soldier, one who has gone against her orders, not as a princess with responsibilities to her people. Well, they have a responsibility to me, too. And I'm doing what I'm doing, not just for Sage, but to make sure the werenation is safe.

At least, I am, now. And with someone like Tallah

to speak on my behalf... this could work. And maybe, just maybe, I can have my throne and the man I love, too.

"Thank you, Tallah." She smiles, hugs me hard. Stranger things have come about in my life since I met Sydlynn Hayle. Who is to say the werenation will turn Sage away if we're able to clear his name, prove he's not a revenant but the next evolution of our kind? I know better than to hope, but I will not write him off.

I love him too much, and this strategy of Tallah's has given me a bright spot to focus on, not just about Sage, but for my entire race. I will drag them into the future. And I'll use diplomacy and shades of gray to do it.

I turn around, heading back outside. Poor Sage, why did I do this to him? Because I wasn't thinking as a ruler, but as someone to be ruled. Time to change that, to truly be Sharlotta. Charlotte is a warrior, bred to serve. No more.

My destiny is my own, tied to my people or not.

Instead of finding my love where I left him, I almost run into Piers as I stride out onto the deck and into the sunshine. He catches me, grinning still, eyes guarded.

"You okay?" He lets me go after an impulsive hug, hands in the pockets of his jeans, angular face frozen in his grin. I can feel his pain oozing from him, but I have no idea how to soften the blow.

"No," I say. "I have to find Sage. And apologize." For being small minded and short sighted. I have so much to learn.

Piers catches my arm, holds me back a moment. I watch him swallow, see the pain transform into acceptance before he bends and kisses my cheek. "We would have been amazing together."

I shrug. "I'm sorry, Piers."

But he's already pulling away, grinning again, though this time, his eyes sparkle with amusement. "I'm not," he says. "That's two bullets I think I dodged. You and Syd, too much to handle, the pair of you."

My fingers brush his cheek. "Whoever wins you at last," I say, "she'll be a lucky woman."

Piers looks away, off over the water, eyes near transparent from the bright sun. "She's out there, somewhere," he says, wistful, sad, before turning back to me with a smirk. "For now, we have another job to do. Find a way for you and wolf boy to be together." He rolls his eyes. "If that's what you really want."

I laugh, hug him hard. "Thank you, Piers."

"You're welcome." He lets me go, turns me toward the sand and the beach. "He went that-a-way."

I leave Piers there, hurry down the steps and trot down the beach, eyes searching the sand for the dark figure of Sage ahead. Maybe we can make this work. We are different, all of us, the werewolves. Syd will think of something or Piers with his clever mind. Tallah with her diplomacy and me, the new me, unwilling to take no for an answer from my obstinate race. My grandfather will soften when he sees Sage is not a typical revenant.

I'll make it happen. A grin breaks over my face. I will make it happen.

I'm so wrapped up in my growing hope and happiness it's several minutes before I realize there's no one down this stretch of beach. Did I go the wrong way? Another quarter hour of searching and fear has replaced my newfound determination.

Tallah and Piers join my worried hunt, but it's clear an hour later, the worst has occurred.

Whether by choice or by force, Sage is gone.

TWENTY-SIX

I hover next to Tallah who gives telepathic orders to her coven while my heart stretches out toward Sage. I can't reach him with my power, and I don't dare push too hard. I refuse to bring the Enforcers down on the Hensley coven after Tallah and her people have done so much for me. They are no longer disposable, but almost as dear as the Hayles.

Funny how things change when you see shades of gray.

Tallah turns to me in full leader mode. "You can't find him?"

I shake my head, lower lip trembling despite my attempt to control my emotions. "He's nowhere," I say, my voice cracking with strain.

Tallah hugs me with one arm, her energy joining

mine, lending me strength. "We'll find him."

"We have to," I say. "He could change at any moment and without me there..." He could turn into a monster after all. Though I don't believe that of him anymore, who knows what he's becoming?

"The entire coven is out looking for him," she says, nodding to Piers who steps out of a black tunnel, concern on his face. "Time you two joined them."

I hug her and run after my sorcerer friend who has just dropped off some witches in the search grid Tallah has designed. He pauses on the deck, offering his hand, opening a new dark way. "I haven't felt a trace of other sorcery," he says. "So I don't think he's been taken, at least not through power."

"That means he left on his own." I want to sob. What have I done to him? I broke his heart, and without exploring all avenues. I'm as bad as my grandfather.

"Maybe." Piers gestures at the opening. "Or they took him through physical means. No matter the reason, we'll find him. After you."

The darkness embraces me, and I hug it back for once. It draws out my emotions as well as pulling at my power and by the time Piers and I emerge into a small alley off a Los Angeles street, I'm feeling more calm, level.

It's almost dark again. Last day. Sage could shift at any moment. The sun sets over the ocean as Piers and I gain our bearings. I reach for Sage's mind again. If he's in the city, if he's made it this far, I might be able to locate him just by proximity.

My mind reaches—and encounters darkness.

Piers spins at the same moment, turning me with him, his power roaring out below us in black flames. I feel my body tighten in response, the wolf in me wanting to surface, but I hold her back at the sight of the two young people watching us.

The guy is tall, almost as tall as Piers, with close-cropped, dirty blond hair and tanned skin. He glares like we're the enemy, though he doesn't move to attack. The girl, on the other hand, gapes at us, a silver lighter raised before her in one slim hand, her huge amber eyes, reminding me of a demon, staring like she's seen a ghost.

"Piers Southway," my sorcerer friend introduces himself. "Charlotte Girard. You're Steam Union?"

The guy flinches, nudges the girl. "Not a chance," he snarls. "Get us out of here."

She twitches, looks up at him, as though only then noticing he's there. "Kayden?"

He pushes her firmly, her hand convulsing around the lighter even as black flames of his own lick across the ground toward us. But I can see and feel he's no match for Piers, not by a long shot, and the girl is still too rattled to be of help.

"We won't hurt you," I say. "We're looking for

someone. A friend. He's in danger and we need to find him."

The girl is still shaken, but she seems to be coming back to herself. "What friend?"

I open my mouth to speak but the guy next to her, Kayden, reaches out and tries to take her lighter. "Now, Zoe!"

She starts, looks guilty and thumbs the lighter into flame. Piers takes a step toward them, the girl's gaze locked on him, before the pair seem to shrink and dissolve, slipping into the flame before it flickers out and is gone.

Piers curses into the growing shadows, turning to me. "I'm going after them." He leaves me there, the dark tunnel of his making devouring him, the end snapping firmly shut.

I'm suddenly lonely, missing Sage, missing my pack. But I've learned to be on my own, haven't I, after years of training, courtesy of Andre Dumont? I shudder past the innate need of werewolves to work in a group, knowing I'm probably better off in this instance.

The streetlights come on as darkness claims the city. I step out onto the sidewalk, eyes settling on a sign just down half a block. A biker bar, from the look of it, with a couple of big Harley Davidson motorcycles out front, a narrow driveway beside. What had Anna said about Caine and his people? That a gang had gone missing?

It was worth a shot. And Piers brought us here for a reason, even if he didn't tell me directly what that reason is.

The heavy door is silent when I pull on it, and I step into heavy smoke. A large man covered in tattoos, most of his chest exposed despite the leather vest he wears, tries to stop me from going further.

"Private club," he says in a voice like the depths of the earth.

"I'm looking for Caine," I say. He grunts like I hit him, glances over his shoulder.

"Not here anymore." He seems less antagonistic, more curious, eyes traveling over me. I know I look like a college girl, a tourist maybe. But when he meets my eyes, I let him see the wolf and he backs off. Yes, it's against our laws. But if he knows Caine, surely this isn't the first time he's encountered eyes like mine.

"I need information," I say. "Anyone here who can help me?"

Big boy nods, steps aside. Points at a lean, older man at the table closest to the bar. Cigar smoke hovers in the air, the scent of marijuana, whisky, and beer married to sweat and leather. "Chokehold," the bouncer says. "Not my problem what happens when you ask."

I shrug and walk past him. The moment I do, everyone stares, the twenty or so occupants of the small bar. It's typical biker chic interior, a giant pool table at one end, the chairs studded and covered in black leather. One of the women scowls at me, her heavily made-up eyes and bleached hair trying for forty and failing miserably. I ignore her, moving with confident purpose to the lean, old man watching my approach with a cigar clamped between his teeth. His long, gray braid sits in his lap, leather cap holding it back from his face. He has so many tattoos on his wrinkled arms I would never sort them out, even if I had the time.

I come to a halt in front of him as he pushes back his chair to look up at me. "Caine," I say, releasing my wolf again, enough he sees what he's dealing with. "Who made him?"

It's possible I'm barking up a dead tree, that I've made a terrible mistake and broken our laws, showing myself to normals for no good reason. But Chokehold's reaction tells me I'm dead on target.

"Caine and his bunch are long gone," Chokehold says in an oddly mild and cultured voice. "But you know that."

I nod. "I'm looking for his maker."

The old biker sits forward, rolling his cigar around in his mouth. "Might be able to point you in the right direction," he says. "You same as Caine?"

I shake my head. "Better."

Chokehold laughs, startling the woman sitting next to him. She's younger, too young, in my opinion, to be hanging onto his every word. But I'm not here to save her.

"I bet you are," he says. "Caine's a jackass."

"We're in agreement," I say. "Can you help me or not?"

Chokehold drops his cigar to the floor and steps on it before slowly rising to face me. He's just my height, slim and lean. Which means he's all kinds of dangerous if he can hold his own against the burly men watching us, no matter his age. I can tell someone like him has proven time and again to be the best, and I will not underestimate him. Just as I can tell by the way he treats me, he will not take my quiet confidence for granted.

"You're looking for someone else." Chokehold crosses his arms over his chest.

My heart skips. Is he talking about Sage? "Maybe," I say. "Young, dark hair?" I shake my head, remembering his current state of disguise. "Dyed blonde?"

He nods. "Asked the same questions you did. Same eyes, too."

Relief, though short lived. Sage left me on purpose then. And I let him go without knowing it. Worse, Sage is turning without support, with Enforcers out there, maybe werewolves, if Caine has tracked us. I have to find Sage and keep him safe until we know our next step. "Where did you send him?"

Chokehold grins at me. "Didn't," he says. "Because

I have no idea." The crowd mutters agreement. "See, Caine and his crew, they weren't the only ones who were offered a deal. But we all said no." Is that fear in his voice? "As in, hell no." More agreement. "In fact, if the dude hadn't looked so nuts, I would have killed him myself."

Dude? Sage? No, not Sage.

"Rupe." I look around. They don't recognize the name, shaking their heads.

Chokehold grunts. "Some scrawny shit in a suit, but pure freaking psycho. Caine's just crazy enough to say yes."

So we were right about who made Caine. Tallah is an expert at supposition. "Liander Belaisle."

"That's the one." Chokehold shrugs. "Sent him off with Cicero and those Knox sibs. Good riddance." It *is* fear.

"They came back." I don't have to look around this time, the confirmation coming in a wave of anxiety.

Chokehold lets his arms fall to his sides. "I've killed lots of people in my life," he says, voice soft, "for good reasons and bad. But I ain't never seen such evil before." He shivers while the others back away. "You don't feel like him. But you're the same."

"Better, I said." I wink. "Much, much better."

"Good enough to take him down?" The old man shrugs. "Whatever." Chokehold gestures at the door. "We told you what we know. Now you get to leave in one piece. And never come back."

His threat might be real, but we both know it's empty. I could kill them all if I chose, and they wouldn't stand a chance against me. But he's given me all he knows, and that has earned my respect.

I wish there was more, but I'm certain Chokehold and his people would have told me, if only to make sure Belaisle never returns.

The street outside is dark and humid as the big bouncer closes the door behind me. At least I now have solid proof Caine is a revenant. I have witnesses who knew him as human, before Belaisle turned him. That's something. I also know the Brotherhood is involved.

And I know Sage is okay and on his own, not under the control of the sorcerers. Until they find him. He can take care of himself in normal circumstances, but this mess is far from normal.

I have to find him. My power snakes out, a thin thread, searching for him, only to encounter more sorcery. The alley where Piers and I arrived is occupied again. But it's not my friend this time.

I cross the street, enter the dark slowly, unsurprised to find the dark-eyed girl waiting for me.

TWENTY-SEVEN

"You recognized me." I close the distance between us though she backpedals slightly, nervous, despite the fact she's the one who came to see me.

"Yes," she says, the hand holding her dead lighter in front of her shaking. Her voice barely rises above a whisper. I come to a halt, not wanting to scare her off, but needing to know what she knows. And who she is, exactly.

"You're Steam Union?" Where is Piers? He obviously didn't find her, off on a goose chase, at this point. Or pursuing the girl's sorcerer friend, more likely. He seemed less inclined to talk to us. What's different about her?

"I don't know what that means," she says, voice

rising a little. She's a lovely thing, delicate and slim, with exotic features that make me think of Greece. "What's Steam Union?"

Well, that's not helpful.

"You're a wolf," she says. "A blonde wolf. But you have blonde hair as a human, too, only it's black right now." She seems confused. "And you travel with her a lot."

I'm immediately tense, hackles rising. What the hell is this? "How do you know me?" I'm certain I've never seen her before. She certainly doesn't smell familiar.

She shivers, fingers adjusting around the silver lighter. She keeps it between us, as though it will protect her from me. But if I want to take her down, I'll be on her before her thumb can strike a flame.

"I've seen you," she says. "My entire life."

My wolf chuffs her confusion. Seen me how? "You're not making any sense." Who is she?

She shakes her head, as though fighting with herself. "You travel with her, you're always with her, I've seen it." Faint horror rises in her huge, dark eyes. She licks her lips, nervous. "I shouldn't be here. But I had to know if it was really you."

"Who are you talking about?" I don't have time for this nonsense. That's what her gibberish sounds like. If she's not Steam Union, she's not helpful. Maybe I'll come back when this is over—if I can—and have a chat with the odd girl before me. But right now, I have to find Sage before it's too late.

"You know who I'm talking about," she says. "The woman with the rainbow magic."

Everything goes still inside me. Syd. She's talking about Syd.

"She's evil, you know." The girl is shaking harder, pupils dilated, eyes frightened. "You have to get away from her. Don't let her hurt you."

Now my anger surfaces, my wolf ready to take her out for the lies she's speaking. What the hell is this? "Syd would never hurt me." I take another step closer, Sage in the back of my mind, but my worry for my friend in Wilding Springs taking over while my wolf surfaces in my eyes. "She's not evil, any more than I am."

The girl wails softly, though she doesn't retreat from me despite my rising anger. "I've seen it," she cries. "I've seen the end of the world, and she's the cause of it."

My heart pounds heavily for a few beats, confusion at war with my temper. "Who are you?"

"My name is Zoe," she whispers. "Zoe Helios. I'm an Oracle. And I've seen everything."

It takes so much effort not to lunge at her, seize her in my hands and shake her, shake her so hard she stops lying about Syd. "Tell me what you've seen."

Awe seems to take her, replacing some of her fear. "I can't believe it's you," she says, wiping at a tear trickling from her big eyes. "All this time, since I was a little girl. I'm finally meeting The Wolf." She says it like she's capitalizing the words, as though it's a title. "And him," she says. "The Sorcerer." She has to be talking about Piers. "That means it's almost time." She sobs softly once before pulling herself together, cheeks wet again. Only this time she doesn't try to dry her tears. "Please, you have to listen to me."

If it's more nonsense about Syd, she can forget it. "Pay attention, child," I say. "I don't have time for your games right now. I'm looking for someone, and unless you can help me find him, you're on your own."

Her mouth opens and closes before she shakes her head. "I can only see the future I've been assigned," she says. "I'm sorry. But you have to stop her." She moves toward me before falling back when I snarl at her. "You have to stop the one with the rainbow magic before it's too late."

I cut the air with one hand. "If you're still talking about Syd," I growl, "you can shut your mouth. She's saved our asses—this whole Universe—so many times I've lost count. You should be damned grateful for her." I can barely control my rage, wanting to let it out all over this tiny thing who makes my head spin. "You're standing here," I spit the last few words, "because of her. So stop talking before I make you stop."

Zoe shakes her head, horror on her face. "No," she

says. "That's not true."

"It is," I say, "and unless you were there, little oracle girl, I'd keep my damned mouth shut. Because I was." I pound my chest with one fist. "I was. I saw it happen, I lived it."

She stumbles back, head dropping. "It's not possible." Her free hand lifts to grasp the lighter, which flickers to life on its own. A flame appears, images flashing. I catch only a few, one of them predominant— Syd's grim face. "I've seen it all!"

"Whatever." I turn my back on her.

"Wait!" She comes after me, stops just behind me as I turn to face her again. She's young, maybe eighteen, earnest and afraid, lost. "She is the Dark One."

"The Dark One," I say, "is dead and gone, at Syd's hand, five years ago." Some oracle this girl is.

The flame rises between us and a face appears in the fire. Syd again. "The Dark One," she repeats.

How has this kid gotten things so confused? "I don't know who is supplying your little prophecies," I say, jabbing a finger at the fire, "but that woman is the Light One, girl."

Zoe's eyes fill with tears, her lower lip trembling. "No," she whispers. "It can't be true. How can it be true?" She stares into the flame. "Is it all a lie?"

I reach for her, she's so distraught, but she begins to fade too quickly, vanishing into the flame, the lighter flickering out and disappearing with her.

Syd needs to know something is wrong. Whoever this kid is, claiming to be an Oracle, she's seen something big coming. I have to warn my friend.

But Sage...I can't risk reaching for Syd now. And there has to be time.

I spin, hunting Sage's scent, and run for the street again, determined to track him down and finish this so I can help Syd. Because I have a feeling she's going to need all the help she can get.

My face slams into a barrier of darkness, the air smothering me before I can react, blackness engulfing me and dragging me screaming into unconsciousness.

I wake slowly, cheek pressed to cold stone, the scent of mildew and rock filling my senses. It's dark, but not the darkness of sorcery, merely a room absent of light. I push myself up, arms shaking, though I'm recovering from the blow that knocked me out. It had to have been magic to drain my entire body so completely.

My eyes adjust, the low light coming from a crack in the far corner outlining the bottom of what has to be a door. It feels damp and cool here, the weight of some structure above me pressing down, the tang of aged moisture on my tongue. A basement? Yes, that makes sense. And the faint taste of fermentation. A wine cellar, perhaps.

But that's not all. My vision is hampered, my wolf rising slowly, as though stunned herself and only now able to focus, taking a moment before I realize why everything in my vision seems to be cut through with horizontal black gaps.

I'm in a cage, iron bars surrounding me, overhead, keeping me from climbing to my feet.

—*I'm a child again, caged on filthy straw, naked, snarling and terrified, my wolf trying to defend me as he opens the door, his hand on his belt buckle*—

I smell him, mixed with memory, and know this is no past come to haunt me, as much as the two mingle together. This is real, here and now, and he has me once again where he's always wanted to keep me.

"Charlotte," Andre's voice oozes from the darkness as I turn and spot him hovering on a stool, cane before him, watching me with glittering eyes. "So lovely to have you again."

TWENTY-EIGHT

Terror, horror, primal fear, all in the heart of a child who can't bear to be here any longer. My wolf bursts from me, throwing herself at the sides of the cage, while I pant and moan and scream at him, at the past and the horrible, horrible future waiting for me in his care.

He laughs, indulgent. "How perfect you are in any form," he says. "But I prefer the woman to the werewolf." Again, I'm hit by power, his magic smothering my wolf and sending her spiraling down, while the girl in me curls in a corner and whimpers. I collapse on my side, my T-shirt and shorts shredded, the pretty underwear Tallah gave me clinging to me, providing at least some decency in this horror show. I know they won't last long if Andre has his way. He likes to see all of me when he works.

Resignation feels like failure. I have to fight.

The door slams open, a wash of wolf-scent carrying to me, breaking the old pattern into a million pieces. The faint taint of revenant cuts away the girl I was, spins me toward the three figures slinking into the room. Caine grins at me, his wolf in his eyes, while mine recovers to lick her wounds and gather her calm. I'm left with something new to fixate on, weakening Andre's psychological hold on me, hands gripping the bars with a ferocity that shocks me.

Andre doesn't seem quite so confident now as I glare at Caine and his two lackeys. Perhaps he senses his error in judgment. But I'm grateful. Seeing my enemies all together removes the feeling of past mixed with present and allows me to remember I'm not the slave girl I used to be.

Viveca is as hateful as ever, Roman glowering. The pair are so pathetic, I ignore them in favor of Caine and his gloating smile, grinning in return and loving how his smirk fades ever so slightly at the sight of my rebellion.

"There now," Caine says, crouching to look through the bars at me, pushing his power over mine, trying to dominate. "Isn't that better? All safe and sound, little princess?"

I snap my teeth at him, laugh in his face. And shove my own magic at him, magic Andre has lost control of.

I'm still in a cage, but that can be rectified. "Come in here with me," I snarl. "I'll show you just what a wereprincess is capable of."

He turns to the glowering werewoman beside him. "You're making Viveca jealous," he says. She looks unhappy with him, turns her head away. Caine ignores her, turns his head to look at Andre. "I hope you plan to share."

The Dumont leader shrugs, standing, cane in one hand, the other brushing imaginary lint from the front of his expensive suit. Is it possible he doesn't sense the loss of control over me? Please, let it be possible. "I might let you have what's left," he says.

Revenge is a dark and dangerous thing. Unless he gives me the means to fulfill it.

"You've been working together all along," I say, hoping to distract Andre, to keep him from thinking of what he might be missing. Of what I now carefully conceal from him. The timing must be perfect. "To capture me. And Sage."

Caine's head whips around. "Clever girl," he says.

"Not so clever," I say. "I figured that out long ago, you moron."

He bares his teeth, but Andre chuckles.

"My dear Charlotte," he says, "don't bait the help."

Caine's hate for Andre shows in his eyes a moment, but he backs off. So this is an unhappy alliance. Even better. Now, how can I use that to my advantage? Because right now, I can use all the advantages I can get.

"Where is Sage?" If they have him already, if they've hurt him…

"We were about to ask you the same question." Andre hits the side of the cage with the silver top of his cane, making me jump. Residual fear remains, but I'll destroy it shortly. And him.

But Andre is second in my thoughts right now. They don't have Sage. Relief floods through me, worries for myself fall away, knowing my love is safe.

"So who is it really pulling your strings, Andre?" If I can keep him talking, he might tell me something important before I tear out his throat. And put off the inevitable. The woman in me wants to end this now. But the girl has uncurled from her place in my heart and her fear is trying to take over again. She doesn't want to think about what will happen when we are alone with him. "Is it Liander Belaisle? Or his little protégé?" Focus, Charlotte.

Andre's eyes narrow. Damn him, I've hit the mark. He's working with the Brotherhood. Wait until Syd finds out. The Dumont family will be no more. That is, if I'm able to reach her. And if there is anything left of him when I'm done. My little girl whimpers, tries to hide again. I have to release her or this will end badly.

I reach out, searching for Syd, but the moment my

magic touches the ceiling, it's muffled, suppressed. So I'm being shielded. Which means no messages out, no chance of rescue. But Andre has left me access here, in this room, trusting his power is enough to control me.

We'll see about that. Right before I break out of here. I guess I'm going to have to rescue myself.

Caine snarls at me. "Belaisle abandoned us," he says before Andre can cut him off.

"Shut up, you imbecile," Andre snaps. Caine growls under his breath, his two cronies echoing him, but Andre doesn't pay attention to their threat. "I have no idea what you're talking about," he says. "I merely hired Mr. Caine and his pack as my bodyguards, nothing more."

"Against the will of the wereking," I say.

Caine laughs out loud, like what I've said is funny. "We encouraged him to change his mind."

Why do those words make a chill run down the back of my neck?

"Now you know," I say to Andre, "that Belaisle made Caine and his pack into weres—that they are revenants," the three snarl at me, "you are law-bound to turn them in to the Enforcers."

"Oh, my very dear," Andre says, "but I always knew." He gestures at Caine. "I was the one who recruited them from California, who encouraged their intrepid leader to pursue your hand. Who taught them pack law."

"You did a terrible job," I say.

Andre smirks. "No matter," he says. "I may not have been able to educate them well enough to counter your grandfather, but that part of the equation will take care of itself in short order." What does he mean by that? "Now," he turns to Caine while my mind tries to fight my fear for Oleksander, "if you don't mind, I'd like a moment alone with our darling Charlotte. She's been out of my care for so long," he turns back to me, eyes intense and eager, cane slapping against his free hand, "and is in desperate need of reeducation."

My stomach collapses into my feet, heart skipping a beat. The little girl wails, snarls in savagery, feral and wild and terrified. No, please, don't go, stay with me, save me from him—

Caine grins at me, thumbs his nose, laughs. Roman follows him, but Viveca lunges forward and crouches, her face in mine. "I hope it's agony," she says, licking her lips. "But not too much. I want there to be something left over for me to hurt when he's done."

"Viveca." Caine's sharp voice jerks at her like a leash. She rises from her crouch and turns in a lithe movement, leaving me behind. The door shuts with a solid thunk, a flare of blue light appearing over my cage as Andre wakes a witchlight.

"Now then," he says. "Where did we leave off all those years ago?"

TWENTY-NINE

I gasp a breath as the door to the cage opens. But not in fear. Viveca has given me a gift, scattered the child in me, driven her back.

The rest of the shielding around me breaks. The fool, he's bundled his protections around my magic into the seal on the door, failing to create a ward around me personally. So arrogant, forgetting he can no longer order me to do what he wants, the controls of the sorcery that created me, the dark magic of the Black Souls long gone. He's more a fool than I thought.

The girl in me whispers her disbelief while my wolf chuffs in satisfaction. The fear in my heart breaks at last, the child seeing the truth, the pathetic creature Andre is, preying on one so young and without the ability to fight back. She understands this is her chance, a chance she never had. And turns utterly savage.

His power reaches for me, too late. I see the terror on his face, the tables turned, as I lunge from the cage, my own magic surging forward and into him, carrying him back to the ground. He lands hard, crying out, my werewolf shape leaping forward, landing lightly on his chest.

"Andre," I breathe into his face, the magic I control filling me with savage joy as I realize the hold he's had over me is broken forever. No matter what he does to me, no matter if I'm ever in this position again, I will never fear him. The girl in me screams her defiance and sobs her victory.

He gasps for breath, eyes huge. "Please, Charlotte, have mercy." The coward. I've feared him for so long, that fear ingrained in my every cell. And now, here we are, and I can finally put an end to him forever, ensure he never, ever, touches another little girl. I can feel his power worming its way around me, trying to break through mine. He might be a coven leader, but I have the power Syd gave me and enough determination to crush his heart.

"Mercy," I say, bending close so my teeth hover over his throat. "One bite, Andre. One is all it will take and you'll be hunted for the rest of your pathetic little life."

He croaks in fear, magic faltering. "I'm a witch," he

squeaks. "I can't be a revenant."

"So the legends say," I whisper huskily, a drop of saliva falling from one canine to pool in the hollow of his neck. "But I'd like to experiment first hand. Just to be certain."

Andre quivers, moaning in fear. "I beg you!"

"Like I begged you?" I lean back, fury so powerful I can barely contain it. "No, wait. I never once begged, did I? No matter what you did to me. Never once." His hate is in his eyes, enough I know he's still fighting for a way to free himself. Like that will happen. Not now I have him here, in my control. "And that's why you want me, isn't it? Because you couldn't break me. And it drives you mad."

Andre hits me hard with energy, but I'm ready for him, absorbing what I can, deflecting the rest. My claw lashes out, catches his handsome, aristocrat's face along the line of his cheekbone, through the soft flesh of his cheek, under the line of his jaw. Four parallel slices, deep enough to scar, fed with magic to make sure they never, ever heal.

He howls in agony, an animal struggling under me. My wolf pants, sensing prey, wanting to kill him, to end this hunt, but I push her down. Not yet. I will have my pleasure from him first.

Something rumbles overhead, pulling me out of my attention to his pain. Andre collapses under me, passed out from the agony, but I'm not focused on him anymore. Not when another rumble shakes the stone above, dropping a fine mist of dust over us. I climb from his silent body, werewolf shape carrying me silently to the door. It's locked, but my magic is enough to open it, now Andre's magic no longer binds it closed. The moment I touch it, another massive thud echoes down from upstairs, the ground under my feet vibrating from the power.

A battle goes on above me. But who is fighting? I glance back at Andre, passed out, bleeding, and make a choice to leave him behind. He's not going anywhere, not worth further effort or consideration. Not when I have a fight to investigate.

The door opens into a stone corridor, ending in a blank wall on one end, a set of stairs on the other. I glance through a partially open space, see a wine cellar. So I was right, this is a basement. My paws are silent on the stone as I climb, turning to wooden stairs and a finely wrought handrail of black-painted iron. I reach the top, the main floor, in a giant kitchen. This has to be an estate of some kind, perhaps a winery, the kitchen appearing industrial. My power reaches out, seeking those who fight, and encounters a familiar dose of magic.

Charlotte! Tallah's mind grasps onto mine. *You're all right!*

I'm here. I feel the pressure of black emptiness as

Piers latches onto me.

I'm going to kill whoever did this, he snarls, *then resurrect them and kill them again.*

It's fine, I send. *I'm okay. It's the Dumonts and Caine's pack.*

We know. Tallah's mind shows me the fight, the pack now in retreat through what looks like a vineyard, into the hills beyond. *Where are you?*

In the main house, I'm guessing, I send. *I'm coming to you. Andre is below. You might want to send someone to make sure he doesn't bleed to death.*

Tallah's hesitation ends abruptly. *If you say so*, she sends.

I slip past the huge island with the stovetop and giant sinks, most of me with Tallah and Piers. It's not until I hear a soft chuff of air I realize my mistake, the scent of her reaching me an instant before Viveca's claws whistle over my head.

I roll, tucking myself forward, sweeping out my own claws toward her legs. She howls her fury, leaping for me, jaws open, her werewolf form foaming at the mouth. I hit her hard in the breast bone as she tries to land on me, power taking her full in the chest, sending her back to crash into the island, sliding across the slick surface of the stove and over the other side.

My paws scramble over the ceramic tile floor, seeking purchase as I crouch, preparing to leap. She beats me to it, surging up and over the island, both clawed hands out, her own magic formed into a shimmering hammer before her. I dodge to the right, spinning to grasp her hips and increase her momentum, shoving her forward into the heavy wooden table and chairs at the other end of the room. She crashes headfirst into the old oak, collapsing, shaking her head from the stunning blow.

The door to the room bursts open, Piers flying through, face frantic. "Charlotte!" I glance up, startled by his appearance. Viveca lurches to her feet and lunges for him.

"Piers!" I cover him with power, shoving him to the side as she flees out the door and is gone. "Damn it!" I have to go after her, finish the fight. But as I try to pass, Piers grabs me, pulls me back, his sorcery quieting my wolf, reverting me to human shape. I snarl at him for his presumption, but he pulls me to him and hugs me before I can give him hell.

"I'm so glad you're okay." His voice chokes in fear. "We thought..." He doesn't finish, leaning back to stroke hair from my face.

"You idiot," I say, though the force of my anger is gone, partly because I'm so scantily clad and aware of Piers's attention. "I could have finished Viveca."

"No time," he says, turning and gesturing, a black tunnel opening beside him. Only then do I feel the pressure of Enforcer magic coming toward me. "Tallah's holding them off, but we have to go."

We're about to step through when the mind I love touches mine.

Charlotte—

Sage! I reach back, resisting Piers who shakes his head, fear returning.

"We need to leave now." He tries to force me toward the tunnel, but I let him feel Sage.

"He's close." Very close. And, from the wavering feeling of him, the way my wolf reacts to him, he's changing. Sage is finally changing and I'm not there to help him.

Piers grits his teeth, then nods. "Show me where."

The tunnel wavers, the blackness rippling as I connect the touch of Sage with Piers. This time I go eagerly, leading my friend toward the man I love. I stumble out of the tunnel into the dark night, in the California hills, to the feeling of Sage and his wolf becoming one.

"This will draw the Enforcers," Piers says. "I'll lock him down as best I can, but no promises, Charlotte."

I'm running already, following Sage's touch, reaching for him with my heart, my mind. He embraces me, his soul altered, flickering between man and wolf.

Charlotte! Tallah's voice reaches me, but it's faint. *Piers is doing his job. I can't hold them off forever.* The Enforcers are coming, then. *Let Piers take him somewhere.*

No, not this time. This is my job. I stop abruptly, Piers running into my back. I ignore him, my magic gathering, reaching for the veil. Sage is close, but not close enough, I won't reach him by foot before the Enforcers track us down. There's only one way.

I reach behind me and take Piers's hand. "Hang on," I say. And tear open the veil.

THIRTY

This time, I don't step into the veil at all, but through the gap cleanly, as though Syd herself made the way. I feel my power drain from me as I do, the fire element in my soul feeding the cut in the veil. I know Syd said my wolf is tied to fire, and I wonder if this is the cost of having such power—losing it to the space between planes.

No matter, I'll pay it, no matter the price. I sag against Piers as we exit the other side, his strong hands holding me up. We're in a small grove of trees at the base of a hill and when I turn around to look, I see the faint flare of blue fire miles in the distance.

"Nice job," Piers says. "But we still have to hurry."

I turn and stagger toward the feeling of Sage, so

powerful now. I had thought him strong when he touched me before, but I had no idea what strong was. What is he becoming, the man I love, that he has this much magic as a revenant?

I trip over a root, almost fall, but for Piers, and finally spot Sage. He's crouched by a tree, and he's not alone. A small pack of timber wolves circle him, panting and whining, their alpha turning to watch me approach. They don't interfere, but I feel their concern.

Sage looks up, his eyes lost to the wolf, his mouth pulled forward into a muzzle. He whines softly, his pain coming through, though his magic surges in waves so strong I know Piers won't be able to mask him for long. I hurry forward, falling to my knees only feet away, knowing I can't interfere beyond offering him energy for support. His body is lost to the change, and there's nothing I can do to stop it.

No, not stop it. But I can do the opposite.

"Piers," I say, tightening my jaw against my fear, "mask this the best you can." I don't wait for him to question what I am about to do. Because if he does, I'll join him in asking if I'm insane, and what's happening to Sage has to be over quickly.

I pour what magic I have left, the strength remaining me, into Sage, feeding his wolf. "Finish it," I say. "Now."

He shrieks into the night, his body shifting, twisting,

clothing tearing from him. His skin morphs into wereform, bones rearranging. Fur grows thick and black on his hide. His ears perk, shining white teeth flashing in the moonlight as his scream of agony turns into the howl of a wolf.

Blue flashes of light surround us, but it's too late. Sage is changed. More than changed. His power settles around him, the werewolf he's become further along the path to pure lupine than any I've ever seen. And still, he is shining and beautiful and pure. He's not a revenant. Sage is something else entirely after all.

I look up at the Enforcers the moment Tallah and her coven appear in their own flares of blue light. A full shield drops around us, blocking us from the black-robed warriors of the Council. She blazes with power, jabbing a finger at a familiar face as Pender slips back his hood, sad eyes on Sage.

"You will not!" She pushes him back in a flash of magic. "They are under my protection!"

A hand falls on my bare shoulder, the touch of Piers stopping my protest. They will hurt Tallah for her disobedience, harm her coven. I can't let that happen. But Sage has padded closer, his black paw settling on my shoulder and the darkness of a sorcery tunnel is already engulfing me.

Blue power slams into the tunnel. Not harming it, but feeding it. I feel the flames swell in answer. But it throws Piers off, enough we are tumbled from the other end and into a dark parking lot, almost crashing into the side of an SUV.

"Come on," Piers says, dragging me to my feet. I grasp for Sage, see he's still in wereform. He seems incredibly calm and composed, despite his furry self, and the power wafting around him. Piers leans into the SUV, popping open the driver's door, slipping behind the wheel. I pull open the back, stuff Sage inside, closing it behind him before circling the car. Piers shoves open the passenger door and I join him in the front, to give Sage space. He's huge, hulking with his shoulders pressing to the ceiling, though his wolf eyes laugh at me, tongue lolling out the side of his mouth.

"This isn't funny," I tell him, while he laughs in my head.

No, Charlie, he sends, as if from a great distance, *this is awesome.*

The tires squeal as Piers pulls out of the parking lot, an attendant waving frantically at us.

"Way to steal a car without being noticed," I say with a dry cut to my voice, shivering a little as the air conditioning blasts my near-nakedness with icy breath.

"Didn't have a lot of choice," Piers grates back through gritted teeth. "The Enforcers will be here any second."

Let them deal with the cops, I guess. "Can't you just

take us out of here?"

Piers shakes his head, taking the corner too tight onto a side road. We seem to be somewhere outside Los Angeles, if just barely. A look out my side mirror shows the city stretched out behind us as we drive into the dark night, up a steep road surrounded by hills and scrub trees.

"Mum's here," he says, his anger finally reaching me. "She tracked me, the bitch, despite my attempts to keep her out. And she'll follow us wherever we go."

Damn it. "I could try to open the veil again." The very thought makes me weak. But I have Sage, his power. He's much stronger than I am right now, probably enough to move us through the veil.

"You think I haven't thought of that?" Piers draws a deep breath, panic in his voice. "They know what your magic feels like now, thanks to Mum." He slams his hands on the steering wheel. "She's been playing me all along, Charlotte. I'm sorry." He shakes his head. "I'm a liability and always have been."

"It's not your fault." I cover one of his hands with mine. "You've been a huge help. Thank you." We would never have made it this far without him.

Piers relaxes a little. "We'll just drive for a bit," he says, "stay low. No magic use." He looks in the rear view mirror. "Get me, wolf boy?"

Sage grunts softly, unable to speak he's turned so far. I worry, but he's not in full wolf form, hovering in well-advanced werewolf shape, so he's still in there, at least.

"You have to get through to Syd." Piers glances at me. "She's your last hope."

"Demonicon." I shudder at the thought, but Piers is correct. "We have to get off-plane."

He nods. "Once you're gone and everyone calms the hell down, maybe we can salvage this. Prove Sage isn't dangerous." He looks back again, through the mirror. "Are you?"

Sage chuckles, a half-wolf, half-human sound.

"I take that as a no," Piers says. "Let Tallah and me deal with Caine and Rupe. Prove that they were made. Get them out of our hair, at least. Then deal with the rest of it. Syd will keep you posted and bring you back when everything's decided."

I hate leaving things to others. It goes against my entire nature. But we've done all we can. And now Sage is turned, there's no way I'll hide him from the Enforcers— or other werewolves—for long.

Fire flares behind me, the heat of it making me jump. I spin as Sage rumbles a growl to find Zoe Helios perched on the bench seat behind him. She stares at him, though she doesn't seem as afraid as I figured she would be, before turning to me. Piers lets out a sharp bark of protest, the car swerving a moment before he pulls it back under control.

"What the bloody hell!" His white knuckles stand out from his grip on the wheel.

"I'm sorry," she says, leaning forward toward me, not flinching from the fact I'm in my bra and underwear. She doesn't even seem to notice. "I didn't mean to scare you. But I had to talk to you again." Desperation ages her. "It can't be true, what you said, about the Light One. The Dark One." She shakes her head, fingers grasping for mine. Her skin is cold, flames flickering behind her dark eyes. "It can't be." But she sounds like she's not protesting as much as mourning what she thought she knew.

"Piers, Zoe Helios. Zoe, you already met Piers. And this is Sage." She nods to my sorcerer friend behind the wheel, then to the werewolf beside her as if he's of no consequence. "Zoe seems to think Syd is the bad guy."

Piers snorts a nervous laugh. "Only if you piss her off by hurting someone she cares about."

Zoe's eyes never leave mine as she leans closer. Her hand is suddenly hot, fire under her skin as she holds me in place. "I've seen you and the ones around you my entire life," she says. "I've watched your story unfold. But I was told you were for the Dark. That everything you did—everything you are to do—will mean the end of the world."

"Whoever told you that," I say, calm and strong, "has been lying to you, Zoe."

236

She flinches. "That doesn't matter," she whispers, looking away. When she lifts her gaze to me again, the flames roar in my mind, scorching the edges of my consciousness. But I stay with her as she speaks. "I see a future for you, Charlotte Girard, Sharlotta Moreau." I start when she speaks my other name. "A future you must avoid at all costs."

"Why are you helping me?" My fingers are on fire, but I won't let go. "I thought I was the enemy?"

She sighs out fire, lost in the flames. "I don't know what to believe anymore," she says. "So I offer this warning. Do not go home. No matter what anyone tells you, what you hear. You must endure, and you will. You are more than strong enough." I'm burning up, she's killing me with flame, but I must hear the rest. "You could avoid the coming trauma, but if you go home now, the werenation will be enslaved once again. Forever."

Zoe pulls away, crying out as I scream from the pain of the fire. But when I look down at my hand, it's fine, unblemished, and the connection to my mind severs, leaving me intact. Zoe

pants, steaming, in the back seat, the flames still in her eyes.

"Heed me," she says. "Or see the end of your people."

I lean toward her. "I need to know more." What is happening at home? The memory of Caine's little comment about my grandfather makes fear spike in my heart. "Tell me more!"

Zoe shakes her head, the flames gone, her hand fumbling for her lighter. "I've told you all I can," she says. She hesitates one last moment, staring at Piers before striking the flame and disappearing into it, gone in a flash of fire.

THIRTY-ONE

I spin on Piers, terror taking hold. "What is she talking about?" I grasp at his arm, almost causing us to go off the side of the road. Piers swears softly and shoves me away while Sage growls in the back seat, anxiety rising with mine.

"Leave off, Charlotte." My sorcerer friend's face is grim.

"You know what she means." I sink back into my seat, fear clawing at my insides like my wolf trying to escape. "Tell me." He's quiet, so quiet. I hit him with all my strength, my human strength, and he shouts in pain.

"Stop it!" He glares at me. "Just stop it."

"Tell me." I glare right back.

Piers shakes his head, running one hand in a shaking

gesture over his hair. "I'm sorry," he says. "I tried to keep it from you. There's nothing you can do, not if you want to save Sage."

"Tell me." For the third time I order him, this one in a whisper.

Piers draws a trembling breath. "Your grandfather is in prison. Awaiting execution."

No. What? Why?

"He refused to declare you a traitor," Piers says, Sage groaning in the back seat. "He tried to block the pursuit." He glances at me, almost shyly. "Caine used his reticence against him, leveraged him off the throne and into a cell."

"Was there a battle?" Piers might as well have punched me in the chest.

He shakes his head, blond hair slipping over my bare leg. "Caine convinced the others to denounce Oleksander," he says.

My teeth squeak as they grind together. "Then his dethroning isn't legal," I say. "Were law dictates he can only be overthrown in battle."

Piers shrugs. "Whatever the truth," he says, "your grandfather isn't king anymore."

Oh, yes, he is. "You're certain he's still alive?"

Piers's hands slip on the steering wheel. "He was the last I heard."

Why would Caine keep Oleksander alive? My wolf

latches on to logic and reason to protect me from my fear. I've put my grandfather in unspeakable danger, assuming he would be fine without me, that he would weather even this storm. I didn't think for a single moment Oleksander's position and life would be at risk.

Piers grunts softly. "He still has some time, if Maks and Isabelle have it right. A few days, anyway. Caine is waiting for others to gather."

He called a pack meeting? We didn't even do that when Oleksander took the throne. "There's only one reason Caine is calling such a gathering."

Piers doesn't answer as I savagely kick the dash of the SUV.

"We have to go back." I can barely breathe. "We have to go to Ukraine and free my grandfather." This is all my fault. If Oleksander dies…And Caine, on the throne, convincing the pack meeting he should be the next wereking…

"That doesn't matter," Piers says. "And if your little friend is to be believed, going back is the last thing we should do."

"Caine." I sob his name. "Caine will be wereking." My heart is crumbling inside me, breaking into so many pieces it will never recover, because I have done this. I have given over my grandfather to his death and my nation to a revenant who is owned by a sorcerer and a despicable witch.

"Charlotte." Piers reaches for me. "Listen to me."

But I can't hear him, there's nothing to hear. I've betrayed them all when I only wanted to save one man. The man I love.

Sage howls in the back seat, his power rippling and it takes me a long moment to realize he's not reacting to my pain. I turn toward him, heart crushed, to see him struggling, clawing at his face as his power continues to flex.

"Charlotte, control him!" Piers swerves as Sage hits the back of his seat with his full weight. The SUV tips dangerously as the front end skips across the pavement. I throw magic at Sage, trying to contain whatever is happening to him, but it's too late, I'm too late.

Sage's power explodes outward, sending the car spinning into the ditch.

Metal screams, twists sideways, sparks flying as I lurch forward and then back, head impacting the glass window before rocketing forward first then back and into the head rest. Metal screams protest, rubber bursting from the strain, the scent of charring plastic and over taxed steel an assault as much as the blows I take.

Darkness sucks away the edges of me.

The SUV thuds to a sudden halt, tipping on its side. I crash into Piers, then the roof as it turns over, then the other side. Piers hangs from his seat belt, unconscious, blood running down his face as the wreck comes to a halt. The back door wrenches from its hinges as Sage tears it free and leaps into the night.

My head aches, though my wolf is already healing me. I can't leave Piers, but Sage is out there and something terrible is happening to him. I have caused so much hurt and loss already, what's one more life on my hands?

Tallah! I throw her name at her with a pulse of magic. She catches me immediately.

Charlotte, where are you? I can feel her moving rapidly closer. Instead of answering, I show her Piers.

Take care of him. And then I cut her off, and leap into the back seat, out the door into the night. I might not be able to save my grandfather, but I'll be damned if I've come this far only to lose Sage.

THIRTY-TWO

I shift as I hit the ground, welcoming my wereshape, the strength it gives me, the supportive embrace of my wolf. I can't cry or sob or crumble when I'm in this body. I'm strong when I'm a werewolf. The weakness of my human skin I leave behind as I race through the California hills after Sage.

He's easy to track, I know him so well, even if his scent wasn't so strong. His energy trails behind him like a flaring beacon. I cut off as much as I can from outside touch, muffling the feeling of him with my own power, though the Enforcers, I'm sure, will find us shortly. They have to. There's no way they can miss the pulse of what is happening to him.

And what is happening? I can't tell, he's too far

beyond me though I'm gaining, from the feel of him ahead. He's struggling with something as his magic shivers and shifts, almost like his body did. The ground flies beneath my paws as I push myself harder than I ever have to reach him. To be with him when whatever is coming completes itself.

I have to catch him before the Enforcers do. It's all I can focus on, the only thought in my head while my body runs on autopilot. They might catch us, but they will find us together, Sage and me. And then, come what may.

Just please, please, if there is a Universal mind out there listening, if Creator can hear me and cares even a little, please don't let him turn into a monster. Because if I have to kill Sage, I will die next to him.

I almost stumble over him when he collapses in a heap at the edge of a forest. He's been running for the trees all this time, our haunt, we wolves. I help him up as he shakes, shivering and twisting in pain, guiding him deeper, smothering the outward feeling of his magic. He seems to understand, pushing it down into the earth beneath us. But whatever is happening doesn't stop because I'm there. If anything, it draws on me and speeds up.

Sage collapses another thirty yards into the forest, whimpering, clawing at the ground. I stop and pant, watching him, dying inside. Is this it? Will he break and will I be forced to kill us both? I will not live without him.

It's been a good life, though fraught with loss and darkness. But I found the light in the end, and I cling to that. I found Syd and her family. I found freedom for mine. And I love Sage.

It will have to be enough.

He looks up at me, eyes full of agony, but without insanity. If anything, they brim with his wolf. A gasp tears from my chest as his magic shifts one last time, and I understand where it is taking him, worse than any madness, beyond the horror of a revenant and out of my arms forever.

Sage sighs as his body shrinks and reforms, the last tatters of his clothing—shredded when he took werewolf shape—fall from him as the wolf inside him takes over completely and he falls into full lupine form. He shakes himself, like a dog emerging from the water, thick black ruff a mane at his throat. I see a white crescent on his left shoulder, the scar of the bite that has, at last, taken the Sage away from me.

Where once there was my love, now there is only a wolf.

He takes a wobbly step toward me as I allow my own wolf to retreat, finding myself naked and shaking, crying at last. Sage sinks to his haunches, licking his chops before trying again. He reaches me this time, butting me with his big head, tongue sweeping across my cheek.

I reach out for him, bury my hands in his fur, my

face in his mane, and weep for his loss. No longer a danger to me or anyone else, he is now a simple beast.

The man I love is gone forever.

Charlie? Am I dreaming? Imagining his voice in my head? I must be. But there it is again, stronger, clearer. *Charlie.*

I lean away, gaping at him, staring in shock. "Sage?" His name barely clears my lips and he licks me again, joyfully.

Hey, Charlie, he sends. *This is awesome. You have to try it.*

I choke a laugh, a sob, hug him so hard he whines but doesn't pull away. "Sage!"

It's weird. He cocks his head to one side, ears perked, dark eyes glistening in the moonlight. *I can feel me, you know? But I'm a wolf.* He snaps his teeth, grinning. *So cool, you have no idea.*

I stutter before I can get the words out, my lips to work well enough. "Change back." Maybe this is a gift, a chance to save him. He's not all gone yet. If he can push himself into wereform, maybe we can keep his mind intact.

Sage shakes his big head, power fluctuating. *Can't*, he says. *Already tried. It's like I'm locked in here, like I was locked in my human body.*

"If you stay like this," I can't stop crying, "you'll lose your humanity." Weres who take full wolf form are lost to us forever, their minds gone to the animal they become.

He shakes again, cold, wet nose on my cheek. *I don't think so*, he sends. *But I guess we'll find out.*

I lean into him, hand still buried in his fur. "I guess we will." I've failed, but he's still with me. Tallah mentioned shades of gray. This is definitely one of those. Any other werewolf would assume he was gone, Sage's mind disappeared into the wolf, no matter his ability to communicate. I just have to see what this means, where this new Sage takes us. But I still have to protect him from those who would kill him for what he's become. Still doomed to death because of the means of his creation.

Revenant. Full form wolf. The man I love.

It's been a very long week.

Sage moves beside me, body warm and strong, his scent mingling with the wolf he's become. It's a good thing. I barely believe this has happened. It's solid proof he's still with me. *The crash*, he sends. *Are you okay?*

I gasp, lean away. I forgot all about the wreck, about my sorcerer friend trapped inside. My legs tremble as I stand.

"We have to find out what happened to Piers." Guilt rides me, drags me forward. Sage stays with me, leaning against me for comfort, his fur warm. I shift into wereform, no longer chilled and naked, and lope back the way we came.

No Enforcers, Sage sends, our power reaching together to feel for the presence of their magic.

I wonder where they could be. How did they miss what Sage went through? I'm grateful. It means we're safe for now. But it's one time I wish they would make an appearance, if only to help the friend I abandoned. *A blessing*, I send. *Hurry*.

We pick up speed, reach the edge of the road faster than I expect. I crouch at the sight of human emergency vehicles, and, at last, the touch of Enforcer and witch power.

They'll take care of him, Sage sends.

I nod, resting my forehead against his fur. Now what? I really don't know. I came here looking for proof of Caine's guilt, only to find he's now wereking, my grandfather deposed. And my search for a cure for Sage has led to him becoming a full wolf.

I've failed far worse than I ever imagined possible.

Don't be silly, Sage sends in a wise voice that's all wolf. *We're not done yet, my love*.

He turns, leads me away from the crash. I follow, though the defeat in my heart makes it hard to put one paw in front of the other.

Sage's heavy head rests in my lap as the boxcar rattles its way over the tracks. I look out the open door over the countryside, trees and water and houses flying by. After a quick theft of clothing for me and a liberated wallet or two for money, we boarded a train heading north. We have nowhere else to turn, nowhere to go. My attempts to reach Syd by magic have done nothing, and my botched tries to reach through the veil have failed. Maybe I need fear or anger or some other powerful boost to push me through. For now, entry to the veil is lost to me.

The black wolf sleeps, grunting softly in his rest, front paws scrabbling a moment at the wooden floor. I stroke his soft ears, tracing the white crescent of the bite on his shoulder, the only evidence remaining of what happened to him. I wish I could offer more comfort. He stills after a moment, the dream of chase over, my fear for him rising. It's a wolf's dream, not a man's. Which means he's losing himself to the creature he's become.

Yes, he's with me now. But for how much longer? I have no way of knowing. He is an anomaly, completely outside my experience. If he is our next evolution, does that mean werewolves are meant to be full wolves instead? But that leads me down a road I can't accept. Like revenant lore, the legend of werewolves who have given in to the full lupine shape tell me he should have lost his humanity already. And I can't believe my people are meant to simply allow themselves to turn to mere animals when we are so much more already.

I think of Femke and the file on revenants. What other information does she have on us that might be relevant? Science and research could say otherwise.

My heart longs to return to Ukraine, to rescue my grandfather. He stood up for me. That fact makes sobs rise in my chest, my throat tightening against them. Even after all I've done, Oleksander loves me and tried to protect me, choosing me over the werenation. Gratitude makes me weep silently for the dear old wolf who I thought had turned his back on me. And I'm just going to leave him there, to be killed by Caine and his people while the false wereking sells us back to sorcerers? I could go back, maybe. Sage is in no further danger from the infection that made him a revenant. I could find a place to leave him, maybe with Syd, or return to California and Tallah.

But if Zoe Helios is to be believed, staying away from home, from the impending death of my grandfather, is exactly what I must do. But can I trust her?

Can I risk not?

And what is this trauma she spoke of? Something I must endure, survive. Whatever it is, I can face it. As long as I have Sage at my side. I stroke his fur again. I will save him. There has to be a way. And this train ride, then another, linked to another, will take me where I need to go.

To her. To Syd. She will save him.

The sun rises in the east, lighting the sky of the eighth day. And I choose Sage. For now. But Cicero Caine and his little pack can watch their backs. Because I will return to my homeland. I will free my grandfather. And if I'm too late, I will avenge him in blood and fire.

Like what you read? Find out more at
pattilarsen.com

Here's a look at the first chapter of
Book Three of Charlotte's trilogy,
The Lychos Cycle

LYCHOS

ONE

The small car smells of cat urine and spoiled milk. I ignore the stench, absorbed instead in the feeling of witch magic pulsing from the tree line before me. A secluded lane more often visited by young lovers offers shelter as I block off my magic even further, just in case.

The big, black wolf shifts beside me, whining softly as his tongue makes a noisy journey across his chops. My fingers find the crescent shape of white fur on his shoulder and dig in. Sage loves it when I scratch the scar, moaning his lupine happiness at the attention, though he is as intent as I am.

I haven't lost him. His mind remains intact, despite his transformation. We've come so far, he and I, the young, normal man I loved first bitten by a werewolf, made a revenant hated and feared by my people. I watched him, in our journey to find a cure to his condition, turn slowly from human to werewolf, without a trace of the tainted darkness that is the revenant's trademark. The very reason my people's werelaws demand his death.

Sage turns to meet my eyes, his still the beautiful sea-green, though with the shape and depth of a wolf's. I can see the man he is inside him still, though I was certain his humanity would be gone forever. When he finally shifted into wereshape in the hills of southern California, just a few days ago, he felt perfect to me, more perfect than any werewolf I've ever met. The Hensley coven leader, Tallah, had surmised he is, rather than a soulless monster to be despised and dispatched, instead the next evolution of the werenation.

I can't help but agree with her. Though we have been unable to reverse his transformation from full wolf back to human, the typical loss of self to animal that usually occurs to us hasn't happened to my darling Sage. I feared that was the case, that I would lose him even when I fought so hard to keep him with me. Gave up everything I loved and the duty and honor my family demanded of me, to save him. It didn't seem fair we'd come so far only for Sage to devolve into the intelligence of a common wolf. Yes, they are brilliant, but they are animals.

My body reacts by scrunching low as I feel an Enforcer's power slip over our hiding place. The guardians of the North American Witch Council have been hunting us since we arrived on the continent. Like her European counterpart, Erica Ployer has caved to the pressure of the werenation, agreeing to hunt us down and deliver us to the less-than-tender mercies of my fellow werewolves. So far, we've managed to elude them, thanks to dear friends and a lot of luck and I won't allow them to capture us now we're so close to ending this.

At least the Enforcers can't see us physically, nor magically, but the impulse to try to hide is too ingrained for me to stop. Sage pants softly next to me, almost cheerful in his demeanor, like this is fun for him.

He always had an odd sense of humor, and even more so now he's a wolf.

Wilding Springs lies beyond the trees. I originally resisted coming here—a place that feels more like home than the palace in Ukraine—in the need to keep my dear friend, Sydlynn Hayle, and her coven out of my mess. She'd been trying ever since Sage and I escaped from the clutches of my people to track me down. At least, she had been. Her touch went silent when Sage and I landed in North America, and I haven't heard from her since.

When I first thought Sage was a revenant, I did my best to keep my friends from becoming embroiled in this disaster, to protect them from my decisions to try to save

Sage. I have no idea what's become of Tallah and her family after the coven leader so openly protected us. Nor of my Steam Union friend, Piers Southway. The last I saw of him, he was unconscious, still in the wreck of the SUV he used to carry Sage and I to freedom. I can't think of them now, though the temptation to wallow in my worry is great.

The worst part is, I now know Sage is no danger to anyone, that he is, in fact, much more than any other werewolf could hope to be. All of this hurt and heartache could have been avoided had I only known in the beginning. Now, I need help to convince the powers that be he is not a threat and to call off the hunt for us.

Sage needs to be safe so I can go home and save my grandfather from execution.

The wolf shifts beside me, leaning in to swipe the side of my face with his tongue. He must feel my anxiety, smell it, because his mind reaches for mine, the barest touch so as not to trigger any power the patrolling Enforcers might pick up on.

We can't sit here all night. Sage's voice is calm, composed, the practical tone of a wolf. My own chuffs her satisfaction at his words. *Any ideas?*

I've assessed and discarded at least a dozen since I pulled in and parked here only fifteen minutes ago. It's been a long journey from California to Pennsylvania and I'm glad to be almost done with it. I need rest—we both do—and anger grinds my teeth together, frustration that the witches in black robes watching over Wilding Springs are keeping me from my destination.

We could just call her out here, Sage sends. *Syd would come in a heartbeat.*

Alerting the Enforcers we're here, I send, scratching his mane with absent fingers. My lower lip hurts from chewing on it, eyes narrowed as I grip the steering wheel with my free hand so tightly my palm cramps. Every scenario I've come up with puts the coven in harm's way. If I can get to Syd and tell her what's happened, find some neutral ground to talk to Femke Svennson, the leader of the European Council, I might be able to diffuse this enough to get Sage a pass so we can go back to Ukraine and make sure my grandfather is safe.

I've been warned to stay away until the time is right, whatever that means. The odd young woman I met in California, Zoe Helios, claims to be an Oracle, to see the future. She warned me against returning too soon, that doing so would mean the permanent enslavement of my people. But according to Piers, Oleksander is under arrest, his execution imminent, all thanks to his support of me after I became a fugitive.

For all I know, Oleksander is already dead. But I refuse to believe it. Regardless my grandfather's state, I will go home and ensure the throne of the werenation never serves as a seat for the revenant pretender, Cicero

Caine. I shudder at the thought of the huge Californian pack leader taking his place where my grandfather should rightfully sit. I can only hope the werenation rejects him as a candidate, and that the gathering of the packs takes far longer than I need to sort out this mess with Sage.

We could just go to the council leader here, Sage sends. *We both know I'm not a danger to anyone.*

I shake my head. *Not an option*, I send. Erica Ployer might be a Hayle witch, but I've never trusted her. Syd's the only one strong enough to keep the peace for any length of time. And she can be very persuasive. Not to mention she's saved the Universe who knew how many times. The magic races owe her.

I owe her.

Another pass of power makes me snarl. Syd can't be home. If she was, she'd be out here, giving these Enforcers grief. I've seen her do it in the past, back when her mother, Miriam, was Council Leader and under the control of the Brotherhood.

Thinking of them makes me even angrier and I need to focus. But it's hard, knowing they are behind this wretched mess, if only by association. Though I have no proof of our guesses and suppositions, the general consensus among my friends is that Caine and his pack are the creation of Liander Belaisle, the leader of the fallen Brotherhood of sorcerers and that his protégé, Rupe, has been trying to recreate what his master made.

New werewolves, the first in centuries. Not since the Black Souls made us have weres been created. Only those born to our lineage are permitted to live. Our bite is viral, infectious, but only to humans, normals. Which leads us full circle to Sage and the reason we're on the run.

I glance sideways at him, hating that my mind always takes this turnabout. The endless cyclical stirring of though leads me from my grandfather to Caine to the Brotherhood and, finally, to Sage and his safety. I'm meant to be werequeen one day, but I can barely keep one wolf safe.

I figure we have a few options, Sage sends. *We can turn ourselves in.*

After all we've been through? We both snort together. Not going to happen.

We can call for Syd. Again, not a choice I'm willing to risk, unless it's absolutely last resort.

We can try to sneak in, Sage sends.

Past all that magic. I sigh and rub my arms with both hands, the thin jacket I stole from the back seat of our liberated car barely enough to keep the September evening chill from my skin. *We might as well just give in*, I send. *They'll be on us the moment we try to cross.*

Even if you take us through the veil? Sage's eyes are so wise, I get lost in them a moment before shaking my head.

Can't, I send, bitterly disappointed by the fact. *We've tried all along, remember? For whatever reason, I can cut into it, but not through it.*

Sage's muzzle dips, forehead pushing against my shoulder. *I think I figured out why.* His nose is cold and wet, but I don't flinch from the touch on my hand. *Remember when you took us to California? When we were being attacked by the hunters?*

I do. It was our only successful jump. Without help, that is. Our first dive into the veil left us stranded in the dark, rubbery membrane between planes. Thankfully a drach had been close by and rescued us. Otherwise I'm certain we would have been lost there forever.

You used me to complete the trip, he sends. My head snaps up as he goes on. *I could feel the drain on my energy, felt you with me. I'm right, aren't I?*

My mouth hangs open a moment before I grasp his furry face in my hands and kiss his snout. *Brilliant*, I send. *Why didn't I think of that?*

I can only guess it's because we were both stressed and tired, Sage sends, practicality tinted with humor. *Can't blame us for forgetting.*

Me, he means. He's so kind, even now.

My wolf reaches for his and finds only Sage. Of course. He's fully integrated, unlike me. When Syd freed my people from the controls of the Black Soul sorcerers who created us, she also freed our magic. But I've always felt a disconnect, as though there are parts of my power I can't yet access. Sage doesn't have that flaw.

More to consider when this is all over and I have time to think.

Can we do it? Sage's magic is ready and willing, a deep and powerful river of deliciousness I wish I could dive in and never emerge from.

I think so. My wolf barks an affirmative. With the boost of his magic, with both of us tied to the demon power Syd claims allows us access to the veil, I'm sure we can make it through.

That still doesn't solve our problem. *They'll feel us use our magic*, I send.

Sage bobs his head. *That's the only downfall*, he sends. *So any way we look at it, we're going to get caught.* He sighs, the hot puff of his breath on my cheek as he licks me. *If only there were some way to hide the power we use.*

The image of a dark and quiet cavern enters my mind, a gasp of air pulling me around to hug Sage close to me. His wolf body quivers as he catches my excitement and when I pull back to grin at him, his tongue lolls out of the side of his mouth in a wolf grin.

You, I send, *are a genius.*

ABOUT THE AUTHOR

Everything you need to know about me is in this one statement: I've wanted to be a writer since I was a little girl, and now I'm doing it. How cool is that, being able to follow your dream and make it reality? I've tried everything from university to college, graduating the second with a journalism diploma (I sucked at telling real stories), am part of an all-girl improv troupe (if you've never tried it, I highly recommend making things up as you go along as often as possible). I've even been in a Celtic girl band (some of our stuff is on YouTube!) and was an independent film maker. My life has been one creative thing after another—all leading me here, to writing books for a living.

Now with multiple series in happy publication, I live on beautiful and magical Prince Edward Island (I know you've heard of Anne of Green Gables) with my very patient husband and multitude of pets.

I love-love-love hearing from you! You can reach me (and I promise I'll message back) at patti@pattilarsen.com. And if you're eager for your next dose of Patti Larsen books (usually about one release a month) come join my mailing list! All the best up and coming, giveaways, contests and, of course, my observations on the world (aren't you just dying to know what I think about everything?) all in one place: http://smarturl.it/PattiLarsenEmail.

Last—but not least!—I hope you enjoyed what you read! Your happiness is my happiness. And I'd love to hear just what you thought. A review where you found this book would mean the world to me—reviews feed writers more than you will ever know. So, loved it (or not so much), **your honest review would make my day**. Thank you!